THE DREAMERS

MYSTERIES FROM WILDSIDE PRESS

Earl Derr Biggers

The Agony Column
Fifty Candles

Michael Bracken

Bad Girls: One Dozen Dangerous Dames
Deadly Campaign
Tequila Sunrise

David Dvorkin

The Cavaradossi Killings
Time for Sherlock Holmes

Joe L. Hensley

Robak's Cross
Robak's Fire
Robak's Firm
A Killing in Gold
The Poison Summer
Song of Corpus Juris
Final Doors
Rivertown Risk
Outcasts

Marvin Kaye

My Brother the Druggist
My Son the Druggist
A Lively Game of Murder
The Soap Opera Slaughters
Bullets for Macbeth
The Country Music Murders

Ray Faraday Nelson

Dog-Headed Death

THE
DREAMERS

Being a More or Less Faithful
Account of the Literary Exercises
of the First Regular Meeting of
that Organization, Reported by

J O H N   K E N D R I C K   B A N G S

A WILDSIDE PRESS MYSTERY CLASSIC

THE DREAMERS

Published by:

Wildside Press
P.O. Box 301
Holicong, PA 18928-0301
www.wildsidepress.com

First Wildside Press Edition:
July 2001

10 9 8 7 6 5 4 3 2 1

CONTENTS

CONTENTS

ILLUSTRATIONS

ILLUSTRATIONS

The Dreamers : A Club-
by John Kendrick Bangs

THE DREAMERS: A CLUB

THE IDEA

THE idea was certainly an original one. It was Bedford Parke who suggested it to Tenafly Paterson, and Tenafly was so pleased with it that he in turn unfolded it in detail to his friend Dobbs Ferry, claiming its inception as his very own. Dobbs was so extremely enthusiastic about it that he invited Tenafly to a luncheon at the Waldoria to talk over the possibilities of putting the plan into practical operation, and so extract from it whatever of excellence it might ultimately be found to contain.

A   1

"As yet it is only an idea, you know," said Dobbs; "and if you have ever had any experience with ideas, Tenny, you are probably aware that, unless reduced to a practical basis, an idea is of no more value than a theory."

"True," Tenafly replied. "I can demonstrate that in five minutes at the Waldoria. For instance, you see, Dobbsy, I have an idea that I am as hungry as a bear, but as yet it is only a theory, from which I derive no substantial benefit. Place a portion of whitebait, a filet Bearnaise, and a quart of Sauterne before me, and—"

"I see," said Dobbsy. "Come along."

And they went; and the result of that luncheon at the Waldoria was the formation of "The Dreamers: A Club." The colon was Dobbs Ferry's suggestion. The objects of the club were literary, and Dobbs, who was an observant young man, had noticed that the use of the colon in these days of unregenerate punctuation was confined almost entirely to the literary contingent and its camp-followers. With

2

DISCUSSING THE IDEA

small poets particularly was it in vogue, and Dobbs—who, by-the-way, had written some very dainty French poems to the various *fiancées* with whom his career had been checkered—had a sort of vague idea that if his brokerage business would permit him to take the necessary time for it he might become famous as a small poet himself. The French poems and his passion for the colon, combined with an exquisite chirography which he had assiduously cultivated, all contributed to assure him that it was only lack of time that kept him in the ranks of the mute, inglorious Herricks.

As formulated by Dobbs and Tenafly, then, Bedford Parke's suggestion that a Dreamers' Club be formed was amplified into this : Thirteen choice spirits, consisting of Dobbs, Tenafly, Bedford Parke, Greenwich Place, Hudson Rivers of Hastings, Monty St. Vincent, Fulton Streete, Berkeley Hights, Haarlem Bridge, the three Snobbes of Yonkers — Tom, Dick, and Harry—and Billy Jones of the *Weekly Oracle*, were to form themselves into an

5

association which should endeavor to extract whatever latent literary talent the thirteen members might have within them. It was a generally accepted fact, Bedford Parke had said, that all literature, not even excepting history, was based upon the imagination. Many of the masterpieces of fiction had their basis in actual dreams, and, when they were not founded on such, might in every case be said to be directly attributable to what might properly be called waking dreams. It was the misfortune of the thirteen gentlemen who were expected to join this association that the business and social engagements of all, with the possible exception of Billy Jones of the *Weekly Oracle*, were such as to prevent their indulgence in these waking dreams, dreams which should tend to lower the colors of Howells before those of Tenafly Paterson, and cause the memory of Hawthorne to wither away before the scorching rays of that rising sun of genius, Tom Snobbe of Yonkers. Snobbe, by-the-way, must have inherited literary

6

ability from his father, who had once
edited a church - fair paper which ran
through six editions in one week—one
edition a day for each day of the fair—
adding an unreceipted printer's bill for
eighty-seven dollars to the proceeds to be
divided among the heathen of Central
Africa.

"It's a well-known fact," said Bedford
—"a sad fact, but still a fact—that if Poe
had not been a hard drinker he never would
have amounted to a row of beans as a
writer. His dreams were induced—and I
say, what's the matter with our inducing
dreams and then putting 'em down ?"

That was the scheme in a nutshell—to
induce dreams and put them down. The
receipt was a simple one. The club was
to meet once a month, and eat and drink
" such stuff as dreams are made of"; the
meeting was then to adjourn, the members
going immediately home and to bed ; the
dreams of each were to be carefully noted
in their every detail, and at the following
meeting were to be unfolded such soul-

harrowing tales as might with propriety be based thereon. An important part of the programme was a stenographer, whose duty it would be to take down the stories as they were told and put them in type-written form, which Dobbs was sure he had heard an editor say was one of the first steps towards a favorable considera-tion by professional readers of the manu-scripts of the ambitious.

"I am told," said he, "that many a truly meritorious production has gone unpublished for years because the labor of deciphering the author's handwriting proved too much for the reader's endur-ance—and it is very natural that it should be so. A professional reader is, after all, only human, and when to the responsibili-ties of his office is added the wearisome task of wading through a Spencerian mo-rass after the will-o'-wisp of an idea, I don't blame him for getting impatient. Why, I saw the original manuscript of one of Charles Dickens's novels once, and I don't see how any one knew it was

8

good enough to publish until it got into print !"

"That's simply a proof of what I've always said," observed one of the Snobbe boys. "If Charles Dickens's works had been written by me, no one would ever have published them."

"I haven't a doubt of it," returned Billy Jones of the *Oracle*, dryly. "Why, Snobbey, my boy, I believe if you had written the plays of Shakespeare they'd have been forgotten ages ago !"

"So do I," returned Snobbe, innocently. "This is a queer world."

"The stenographer will save us a great deal of trouble," said Bedford. "The hard part of literary work is, after all, the labor of production in a manual sense. These real geniuses don't have to think. Their ideas come to them, and they let 'em develop themselves. In realistic writing, as I understand it, the author sits down with his pen in his hand and his characters in his mind's eye, and they simply run along, and he does the private-detective act—follows after them and jots down all they do. In imaginative writing it's done the same way. The characters of these ridiculous beings we read of are quite as real to the imaginative writer as the characters of the realist are to the latter, and they do supernatural things naturally. So you see these things require very little intellectual labor. It's merely the drudgery of chasing a commonplace or supernatural set of characters about the world in order to get 400 pages full of reading-matter about 'em that makes the literary profession a laborious one. Our stenographer will enable us to avoid all this. There isn't a man of us but can talk as easily as he can fall off a log, and a tale once told at our dinners becomes in the telling a bit of writing."

"But, my dear Parke," said Billy Jones of the *Oracle*, who had been a "literary journalist," as his fond grandmother called it, for some years, "a story told is hardly likely to be in the form calculated to become literature."

10

THE IDEA

"That's just what we want you for, Billy," Bedford replied. "You know how to give a thing that last finishing-touch which will make it go, where otherwise it might forever remain a fixture in the author's pigeon-hole. When our stories are told and type-written, we want you to go over them, correct the type-writer's spelling, and make whatever alterations you may think, after consulting with us, to be necessary. Then, if the tales are ever published as a collection, you can have your name on the title-page as editor."

"Thanks," answered Billy, gratefully. "I shall be charmed."

And then he hurried back to his apartments, and threw himself on his bed in a paroxysm of laughter which seemed never-ending, but which in reality did not last more than three hours at the most.

Hudson Rivers of Hastings, when the idea was suggested to him, was the most enthusiastic of all—so enthusiastic that the Snobbe boys thought that, in their own parlance, he ought to be "called down."

"It's bad form to go crazy over an idea," they said. "If Huddy's going to behave this way about it, he ought to be kept out altogether. It is all very well to experience emotions, but no well-bred person ever shows them — that is, not in Yonkers."

"Ah, but you don't understand Huddy," said Tenafly Paterson. "Huddy has two great ambitions in this life. One is to get into the Authors' Club, and the other is to marry a certain young woman whose home is in Boston and whose ambitions are Bostonian. To appear before the world as a writer, which the Dreamers will give him a chance to do at small expense, will help him on to the realization of his most cherished hopes; in fact, Huddy told me that he thought we ought to publish the proceedings of the club at least four times a year, so establishing a quarterly magazine, to which we shall all be regular contributors. He thinks it will pay for itself, and knows it will make us all famous, because Billy Jones is certain to see that everything that goes out is first chop, and I'm inclined to believe Huddy is right. The continual drip, drip, drip of a drop of water on a stone will gradually wear away the stone, and, by Jove! before we know it, by constant hammering away at this dream scheme of ours we'll gain a position that won't be altogether unerviable."

"That's so," said Billy. "I wouldn't wonder if with the constant drip, drip, drip of your drops of ink and inspiration you could wear the public out in a very little while. The only troublesome thing will be in getting a publisher for your quarterly."

"I haven't any idea that we want a publisher," said Bedford Parke. "We've got capital enough among ourselves to bring the thing out, and so I say, what's the use of letting anybody else in on the profits? A publisher wouldn't give us more than ten per cent. in royalties. If we publish it ourselves we'll get the whole thing."

"Yes," assented Tom Snobbe, "and, what's more, it will have a higher tone to it if we can say on the title-page 'Privately printed,' eh? That 'll make everybody in society want one for his library, and everybody not in society will be crazy to get it because it's aristocratic all through."

"I hadn't thought of that," said Billy Jones. "I've no doubt you are right, only I'd think you'd sell more copies if you'd also put on the title-page 'For circulation among the élite only.' Then every man, woman, or child who happened to get a copy would take pride in showing it to others, who would immediately send for it, because not having it would seem to indicate that one was not in the swim."

Nor were the others to whom the proposition was advanced any less desirous to take part. They saw, one and all, opportunities for a very desirable distinction through the medium of the Dreamers, and within two weeks of the original formation of the plan the club was definitely organized. Physicians were consulted by the various members as to what edibles contained the properties most likely to produce dreams of the nature desired, and at the organization meeting all but Billy Jones were well stocked with suggestions for the inauguration dinner. Hudson Rivers was of the opinion that there should be six courses at that dinner, each one of Welsh-rabbit, but varying in form, such as Welsh-rabbit purée, for instance, in which the cheese should have the consistency of pea-soup rather than of leather; such as Welsh-rabbit pâté, in which the cheese should rest within walls of pastry instead of lying quiescent and inviting like a yellow mantle upon a piece of toast; then a Welsh-rabbit roast; and so on all through the banquet, rabbit upon rabbit, the whole washed down with the accepted wines of the ordinary banquet, which experience had taught them were likely in themselves to assist in the work of dream-making.

Monty St. Vincent observed that he had

no doubt that the Welsh-rabbit dinner would work wonders, but he confessed his inability to see any reason why the club should begin its labors by committing suicide. He added that, for his part, he would not eat six Welsh rabbits at one sitting if he was sure of Shakespeare's immortality as his reward, because, however attractive immortality was, he preferred mortality in the flesh to the other in the abstract. If the gentlemen would begin the meal with a grilled lobster apiece, he suggested, going thence by an easy stage to a devilled bird, rounding up with a "slip-on"—which, in brief, is a piece of mince-pie smothered in a blanket of molten cheese — he was ready to take the plunge, but further than this he would not go. The other members were disposed to agree with Monty. They thought the idea of eating six Welsh rabbits in a single evening was preposterous, and that in making such a suggestion Huddy was inspired by one of but two possible motives—that he wished to leap to the fore-

AND SO TO DREAM

most position in imaginative literature at one bound, or else was prompted, by jealousy of what the others might do, to wish to kill the club at its very start. Huddy denied these aspersions upon his motives with vociferous indignation, and to show his sincerity readily acquiesced in the adoption of Monty St. Vincent's menu as already outlined.

The date of the dinner was set, Billy Jones was made master of ceremonies, the dinner was ordered, and eaten amid scenes of such revelry as was possible in the presence of the Snobbe boys, to whom anything in the way of unrestrained enjoyment was a bore and bad form, and at its conclusion the revellers went straight home to bed and to dream.

Two weeks later they met again over viands of a more digestible nature than those which lent interest to the first dinner, and told the tales which follow. And I desire to add here that my report of this dinner and the literature there produced is based entirely upon the stenographer's

notes, coupled with additional informa-
tion of an interesting kind furnished me
by my friend William Jones, Esq., Third
Assistant Exchange Editor of *The Weekly
Oracle, a Journal of To-day, Yesterday,
and To-morrow.*

II

IN WHICH THOMAS SNOBBE, ESQ., OF YONKERS, UNFOLDS A TALE

THE second dinner of the Dreamers had been served, all but the coffee, when Mr. Billy Jones, of the *Oracle,* rapped upon the table with a dessert-spoon and called the members to order.

"Gentlemen," said he, when all was quiet, "we have reached the crucial crisis of our club career. We have eaten the stuff of which our dreams were to be made, and from what I can gather from the reports of those who are now seated about this festal board—and I am delighted to note that the full membership of our organization is here represented— there is not a single one of you who is unprepared for the work we have in hand, and, as master of ceremonies, it becomes my pleasant duty to inform you that the hour has arrived at which it behooveth us to begin the narration of those tales which —of those tales which I am certain—yes, gentlemen, very certain—will cause the unlaid ghosts of those masters of the story-tellers' art—"

"Is this a continued story Billy is giving us ?" observed Tenafly Paterson.

"No," replied Bedford Parke, with a laugh ; "it is only a life sentence."

"Get him to commute it !" ejaculated Hudson Rivers.

"Order, gentlemen, order !" cried the master of ceremonies, again rapping upon the table. "The members will kindly not interrupt the speaker. As I was saying, gentlemen," he continued, "we are now to listen to the narration of tales which I am convinced will cause the unlaid ghosts of the past grand masters of the story-tellers' art to gnash their spirit teeth with anguish for that they in life

22

failed to realize the opportunities that were theirs in not having told the tales to which we are about to listen, and over which, when published, the leading living literary lights will writhe in jealousy."

When the applause which greeted these remarks had subsided, Mr. Jones resumed:

"That there may be no question of precedence among the gifted persons from whom we are now to hear, I have provided myself with a small leathern bottle, such as is to be seen in most billiard-parlors, within which I have placed twelve numbered ivory balls. These I will now proceed to distribute among you. When you receive them, I request that you immediately return them to me, that I may arrange the programme according to your respective numbers."

Mr. Jones thereupon distributed the ivory balls, and when the returns had been made, according to his request, he again rose to his feet and announced that to Mr. Thomas Snobbe, of Yonkers, had fallen the lot of telling the first story,

23

adding that he took great pleasure in the slightly supererogative task that devolved upon him of presenting Mr. Snobbe to his audience. Mr. Snobbe's health was drunk vociferously, after which, the stenographer having announced himself as ready to begin, the distinguished son of Yonkers arose and told the following story, which he called

VAN SQUIBBER'S FAILURE

You can't always tell what kind of a day you are going to have in town in October just because you happen to have been in town on previous October days, and Van Squibber, for that reason, was not surprised when his man, on waking him, informed him that it was cold out. Even if he had been surprised he would not have shown it, for fear of demoralizing his man by setting him a bad example. "We must take things as they come," Van Squibber had said to the fellow when he engaged him, "and I shall expect you to be ready always for any emergency that

24

THE DREAMERS DINE

may arise. If on waking in the morning I call for a camel's-hair shawl and a bottle of Nepaul pepper, it will be your duty to see that I get them without manifesting the slightest surprise or asking any questions. Here is your next year's salary in advance. Get my Melton overcoat and my box, and have them at the Rahway station at 7.15 to-morrow morning. If I am not there, don't wait for me, but come back here and boil my egg at once."

This small bit of a lecture had had its effect on the man, to whom thenceforth nothing was impossible; indeed, upon this very occasion he demonstrated to his employer his sterling worth, for when, on looking over Van Squibber's wardrobe, he discovered that his master had no Melton overcoat, he telegraphed to his tailor's and had one made from his previous measure in time to have it with Van Squibber's box at the Rahway station at the stipulated hour the following morning. Of course Van Squibber was not there. He had instructed his man as he had simply

27

to test him, and, furthermore, the egg
was boiled to perfection. The test cost
Van Squibber about $150, but it was suc-
cessful, and it was really worth the money
to know that his man was all that he
should be.

"He's not half bad," said Van Squibber, as he cracked the egg.

"It's wintry," said Van Squibber's
man on the morning of the 5th of October.

"Well," Van Squibber said, sleepily,
"what of that? You have your instructions as to the bodily temperature I desire to maintain. Select my clothing, as
usual—and mark you, man, yesterday was
springy, and you let me go to the club in
summery attire. I was two and a half degrees too warm. You are getting careless.
What are my engagements to-day?"

"University settlement at eleven, luncheon at the Actors' at one, drive with the
cynical Miss Netherwood at three, five-
o'clock tea at four—"

"What?" cried Van Squibber, sharply.

28

"At fuf—five, I should say, sir," stammered the embarrassed man.

"Thought so," said Van Squibber. "Proceed, and be more careful. The very idea of five-c'clock tea at four is shocking."

"Dinner with the Austrian ambassador at eight, opera at eleven—"

"In October? Opera?" cried Van Squibber.

"Comic," said the man. "It is Flopper's last night, sir, and you are to ring down the curtain."

"True," said Van Squibber, meditatively—"true; I'd forgotten. And then?"

"At midnight you are to meet Red Mike at Cherry Street and Broadway to accompany him to see how he robs national banks, for the *Sunday Whirald.*"

"What bank is it to be?"

"The Seventeenth National."

"Gad!" cried Van Squibber, "that's hard luck. It's my bank. Wire Red Mike and ask him to make it the Sixteenth National, at once. Bring me my smoking-jacket and a boiled soda mint drop. I don't care for any breakfast this morning. And, by-the-way, I feel a little chilly. Take a quinine pill for me."

"Your egg is ready, sir," said the man, tremulously.

"Eat it," said Van Squibber, tersely, "and deduct the Café Savarin price of a boiled egg from your salary. How often must I tell you not to have my breakfast boiled until I am boil—I mean ready until I am ready for it?"

The man departed silently, and Van Squibber turned over and went to sleep.

An hour later, having waited for his soda mint drop as long as his dignity would permit, Van Squibber arose and dressed and went for a walk in Central Park. It was eccentric of him to do this, but he did it nevertheless.

"How Travers would laugh if he saw me walking in Central Park!" he thought. "He'd probably ask me when I'd come over from Germany," he added. And then, looking ahead, a thing Van Squibber rarely did, by-the-way—for you can't always tell by looking ahead what may happen to you—his eyes were confronted by a more or less familiar back.

"Dear me!" he said. "If that isn't Eleanor Huyler's back, whose back is it, by Jove?"

Insensibly Van Squibber quickened his pace. This was also a thing he rarely did. "Haste is bad form," he had once said to Travers, who, on leaving Delmonico's at 7.20, seemed anxious to catch the 7.10 train for Riverdale. Insensibly quickening his pace, he soon found himself beside the owner of the back, and, as his premonitions had told him, it was Eleanor Huyler.

"Good-morning," he said.

"Why, Mr. Van Squibber!" she replied, with a terrified smile. "You here?"

"Well," returned Van Squibber, not anxious to commit himself, "I think so, though I assure you, Miss Huyler, I am not at all certain. I seem to be here, but I must confess I am not quite myself this morning. My man—"

"Yes — I know," returned the girl, hastily. "I've heard of him. He is your *alter ego*."

"I had not noticed it," said Van Squibber, somewhat nonplussed. "I think he is English, though he may be Italian, as you suggest. But," he added, to change the subject, "you seem disturbed. Your smile is a terrified smile, as has been already noted."

"It is," said Miss Huyler, looking anxiously about her.

"And may I ask why?" asked Van Squibber, politely—for to do things politely was Van Squibber's ambition.

"I—I—well, really, Mr. Van Squibber," the girl replied, "I am always anxious when you are about. The fact is, you know, the things that happen when you are around are always so very extraordinary. I came here for a quiet walk, but now that you have appeared I am quite certain that something dramatic is about to occur. You see—you—you have turned up so often at the—what I may properly

call, I think, the nick of time, and so rarely at any other time, that I feel as though
some disaster were impending which you
alone can avert."

"And what then?" said Van Squibber,
proudly. "If I am here, what bodes disaster?"

"'That is the question I am asking myself," returned Miss Huyler, whose grow-
ing anxiety was more or less painful to
witness. "Can your luck hold out?
Will your ability as an averter of danger
hold out? In short, Mr. Van Squibber,
are you infallible?"

The question came to Van Squibber like
a flash of lightning out of a clear sky.
It was too pertinent. Had he not often
wondered himself as to his infallibility?
Had he not only the day before said to
Travers, "You can't always tell in advance just how a thing you are going into
may turn out, even though you have been
through that thing many times, and think
you do."

"I do lead a dramatic life," he said,

quietly, hoping by a show of serenity to reassure her. "But," he added, proudly, "I am, after all, Van Squibber ; I am here to do whatever is sent me to do. I am not a fatalist, but I regard myself as the chosen instrument of fate—or something. So far, I have not failed. On the basis of averages, I am not likely to fail now. Fate, or something, has chosen me to succeed."

"That is true," said Eleanor—"quite true; but there are exceptions to all rules, and I would rather you would fail to rescue some other girl from a position of peril than myself."

That Miss Huyler's words were prophetic, the unhappy Van Squibber was to realize, and that soon, for almost as they spoke the cheeks of both were blanched by a dreadful roar in the bushes beside the path upon which they walked.

"Shall I leave you ?" asked Van Squibber, politely.

"Not now—oh, not now, I beg!" cried Miss Huyler. "It is too late. The catastrophe is imminent. You should

' REMEMBER TO BE BRAVE ' "

have gone before the author brought it on. Finding me defenceless and you gone, he might have spared me. As it is, you are here, and must fulfil your destiny."

"Very well," returned Van Squibber. "That being so, I will see what this roaring is. If it is a child endeavoring to frighten you, I shall get his address and have my man chastise his father, for I could never strike a child; but if it is a lion, as I fear, I shall do what seems best under the circumstances. I have been told, Miss Huyler, that a show of bravery awes a wild beast, while a manifestation of cowardice causes him to spring at once upon the coward. Therefore, if it be a lion, do you walk boldly up to him and evince a cool head, while I divert his attention from you by running away. In this way you, at least, will be saved."

"Noble fellow!" thought Eleanor to herself. "If he were to ask me, I think I might marry him."

Meanwhile Van Squibber had investigated, and was horror-struck to find his misgivings entirely too well founded. It was the lion from the park menagerie that had escaped, and was now waiting in ambush to pounce upon the chance pedestrian.

"Remember, Eleanor," he cried, forgetting for the moment that he had never called her by any but her last name with its formal prefix—"remember to be brave. That will awe him, and then when he sees me running he will pursue me."

Removing his shoes, Van Squibber, with a cry which brought the hungry beast bounding out into the path, started on a dead run, while Miss Huyler, full of confidence that the story would end happily whatever she might do, walked boldly up to the tawny creature, wondering much, however, why her rescuer had removed his shoes. It was strange that, knowing Van Squibber as well as she did, she did not at once perceive his motive in declining to run in walking-shoes, but in moments of peril we are all excusable for our vagaries of thought! You never can tell, when

38

" 'ELEANOR HUYLER HAS DISAPPEARED' "

you are in danger, what may happen next, for if you could you would know how it is all going to turn out; but as it is, mental disturbance is quite to be expected.

For once Van Squibber failed. He ran fast enough and betrayed enough cowardice to attract the attention of ten lions, but this special lion, by some fearful idiosyncrasy of fate, which you never can count on, was not to be deceived. With a louder roar than any he had given, he pounced upon the brave woman, and in an instant she was no more. Van Squibber, turning to see how matters stood, was just in time to witness the final engulfment of the fair girl in the lion's jaws.

"Egad!" he cried. *"I have failed!* And now what remains to be done ? Shall I return and fight the lion, or shall I keep on and go to the club ? If I kill the lion, people will know that I have been walking in the park before breakfast. If I continue my present path and go to the club, the fellows will all want to know

what I mean by coming without my shoes
on. What a dilemma! Ah! I have it;
I will go home."

And that is what Van Squibber did.
He went back to his rooms in the Quig-
more at once, hastily undressed, and when,
an hour later, his man returned with the
soda mint drop, he was sleeping peacefully.

That night he met Travers at the club
reading the *Evening Moon.*

"Hello, Van!" said Travers. "Heard
the news?"

"No. What?" asked Van Squibber,
languidly.

"Eleanor Huyler has disappeared."

"By Jove!" cried Van Squibber, with
well-feigned surprise. "I heard the boys
crying 'Extra,' but I never dreamed they
would put out an extra for her."

"They haven't," said Travers. "The
extra's about the lion."

"Ah! And what's happened to the
lion?" cried Van Squibber, nervously.

"He's dead. Got loose this morning
early, and was found at ten o'clock dying

42

of indigestion. It is supposed he has devoured some man, name unknown, for before his nose was an uneaten patent-leather pump, size 9¾ B, and in his throat was stuck the other, half eaten."

" Ha !" muttered Van Squibber, turning pale. " And they don't know whose shoes they were ?" he added, in a hoarse whisper.

" No," said Travers. " There's no clew, even."

Van Squibber breathed a sigh of relief.

" Robert !" he cried, addressing the waiter, " bring me a schooner of absinthe, and ask Mr. Travers what he'll have." And then, turning, he said, *sotto voce,* to himself, " Saved ! And Eleanor is revenged. Van Squibber may have failed, but his patent-leather pumps have conquered."

III

IN WHICH A MINCE-PIE IS RESPONSIBLE FOR A REMARKABLE COINCIDENCE

WHEN Mr. Snobbe sat down after the narration of his story, there was a thunderous outburst of applause. It was evident that the exciting narrative had pleased his fellow-diners very much—as, indeed, it was proper that it should, since it dealt in a veiled sort of way with characters for whom all right-minded persons have not only a deep-seated admiration, but a feeling of affection as well. They had, one and all, in common with the unaffected portion of the reading community, a liking for the wholesome and clean humor of Mr. Van Bibber, and the fact that Snobbe's story suggested a certain

44

original, even in a weak sort of fashion, made them like it in spite of its shortcomings.

"Good work," cried Hudson Rivers. "Of course it's only gas in comparison with the sun, but it gives light, and we like it."

"And it's wholly original, too, even though an imitation in manner. The real Van Bibber never failed in anything he undertook," said Tenafly Paterson. "I've often wished he might have, just once— it would have made him seem more human —and for that reason I think Tom is entitled to praise."

"I don't know about that," observed Monty St. Vincent. "Tom hadn't anything to do with it—it was the dinner. Honor to whom honor is due, say I. Praise the cook, or the caterer."

"That's the truth," put in Billie Jones. "Fact is, when this book of ours comes out, I think, instead of putting our names on the title-page as authors, the thing to do is to print the menu."

THE DREAMERS: A CLUB

"You miss the point of this association," interjected Snobbe. "We haven't banded ourselves together to immortalize a Welsh rabbit or a mince-pie—nay, nor even a ruddy duck. It's our own glory we're after."

"That's it," cried Monty St. Vincent—"that's the beauty of it. The scheme works two ways. If the stuff is good and there is glory in it, we'll have the glory; but if it's bad, we'll blame the dinner. That's what I like about it."

"It's a valuable plan from that point of view," said the presiding officer. "And now, if the gentleman who secured the ball numbered two will make himself known, we will proceed."

Hudson Rivers rose up. "I have number two," he said, "but I have nothing to relate. The coffee I drank kept me awake all night, and when I finally slept, along about six o'clock next morning, it was one of those sweet, dreamless sleeps that we all love so much. I must therefore ask to be excused."

"WRIT A POME ABOUT A KID"

"But how shall you be represented in the book?" asked Mr. Harry Snobbe.

"He can do the table of contents," suggested St. Vincent.

"Or the fly-leaves," said Tenafly Paterson.

"No," said Huddy; "I shall ask that the pages I should have filled be left blank. There is nothing helps a book so much as the leaving of something to the reader's imagination. I heard a great critic say so once. He said that was the strong point of the French writers, and he added that Stockton's *Lady or the Tiger* took hold because Stockton didn't insist on telling everything."

"It's a good idea," said Mr. Jones. "I don't know but that if those pages are left blank they'll be the most interesting in the book."

Mr. Rivers sat down with a smile of conscious pride, whereupon Mr. Tenafly Paterson rose up.

"As I hold the number three ball, I will give you the fruits of my dinner. I

THE DREAMERS: A CLUB

attribute the work which I am about to present to you to the mince-pie. Personally, I am a great admirer of certain latter-day poets who deal with the woes and joys of more or less commonplace persons. I myself would rather read a sonnet to a snow-shovel than an ode to the moon, but in my dream I seem to have conceived a violent hatred for authors of homely verse, as you will note when I have finished reading my dream-poem called 'Retribution.'"

"Great Scott!" murmured Billie Jones, with a deep-drawn sigh. "Poetry! From Tenafly Paterson! Of all the afflictions of man, Job could have known no worse."

"The poem reads as follows," continued Paterson, ignoring the chairman's ill-timed remark:

RETRIBUTION

Writ a pome about a kid.
Finest one I ever did.

Heaped it full o' sentiment—
Very best I could invent.

50

"I BOUGHT A BOOK OF VERSE"

A REMARKABLE COINCIDENCE

Talked about his little toys ;
How he played with other boys ;

How the beasts an' birdies all
Come when little Jamie'd call.

'N' 'en I took that little lad,
Gave him fever, mighty bad.

'N' 'en it sorter pleased my whim
To have him die and bury him.

It got printed, too, it did
That small pome about the kid,

In a paper in the West ;
Put ten dollars in my vest.

Every pa an' ma about
Cried like mighty—cried right out.

I jess took each grandma's heart,
Lammed and bruised it, made it smart ;

'N' everybody said o' me,
" Finest pote we ever see,"

'Cept one beggar, he got mad,
Got worst lickin' ever had ;

THE DREAMERS: A CLUB

Got my head atween his fists,
Called me " Prince o' anarchists."

Clipped me one behind my ear—
Laid me up for 'most a year.

" 'Cause," he said, " my poetry
'D made his wife an' mother cry ;

" 'Twarn't no poet's bizness to
Make the wimmin all boo-hoo."

'N' 'at is why to-day, by Jings !
I don't fool with hearts an' things.

I don't care how high the bids,
I've stopped scribblin' 'bout dead kids ;

'R if I haven't, kinder sorter
Think 'at maybe p'r'aps I'd oughter.

The lines were received with hearty appreciation by all save Dobbs Ferry, who
looked a trifle gloomy.

"It is a strange thing," said the latter,
"but that mince-pie affected me in precisely the same way, as you will see for

"IT FILLED ME WITH DISMAY"

A REMARKABLE COINCIDENCE

yourselves when I read my contribution,
which, holding ball number four as I do,
I will proceed to give you."

Mr. Ferry then read the following poem,
which certainly did seem to indicate that
the man who prepared the fatal pie had
certain literary ideas which he mixed in
with other ingredients :

I bought a book of verse the other day,
And when I read, it filled me with dismay.

I wanted it to take home to my wife,
To bring a bit of joy into her life ;

And I'd been told the author of those pomes
Was called the laureate of simple homes.

But, Jove! I read, and found it full of rhyme
That kept my eyes a-filling all the time.

One told about a pretty little miss
Whose father had denied a simple kiss,

And as she left, unhappy, full of cares,
She fell and broke her neck upon the stairs.

THE DREAMERS: A CLUB

And then he wrote a lot of tearful lines
Of children who had trouble with their spines;

And 'stead of joys, he penned so many woes
I sought him out and gave him curvature 'f the
    nose ;

And all the nation, witnessing his plight,
Did crown me King, and cry, " It served him
    right."

"A remarkable coincidence," said
Thomas Snobbe. "In fact, the coincidence is rather more remarkable than
the poetry."

"It certainly is," said Billie Jones;
"but what a wonderfully suggestive pie,
considering that it was a mince !"

After which dictum the presiding officer
called upon the holder of the fifth ball,
who turned out to be none other than
Bedford Parke, who blushingly rose up
and delivered himself of what he called
"The Overcoat, a Magazine Farce."

IV

BEING THE CONTRIBUTION OF MR. BED-FORD PARKE

THE OVERCOAT

A FARCE. IN TWO SCENES

SCENE FIRST

Time : MORNING AT BOSTON

Mrs. Robert Edwards. "I think it will
rain to-day, but there is no need to worry
about that. Robert has his umbrella and
his mackintosh, and I don't think he is
idiotic enough to lend both of them. If
he does, he'll get wet, that's all." Mrs.
Edwards is speaking to herself in the sew-
ing-room of the apartment occupied by
herself and her husband in the Hotel

59

Hammingbell at Boston. It is not a large room, but cosey. A frieze one foot deep runs about the ceiling, and there is a carpet on the floor. Three pins are seen scattered about the room, in one corner of which is a cane-bottomed chair holding across its back two black vests and a cut-away coat. Mrs. Edwards sits before a Wilcox & Wilson sewing - machine sewing a button on a light spring overcoat. The overcoat has one outside and three inside pockets, and is single-breasted. "It is curious," Mrs. Edwards continues, "what men will do with umbrellas and mackintoshes on a rainy day. They lend them here and there, and the worst part of it is they never remember where." A knock is heard at the door. "Who's there?"

Voice (without). "Me."

Mrs. Robert Edwards (with a nervous shudder). "Come in." Enter Mary the house-maid. She is becomingly attired in blue alpaca, with green ribbons and puffed sleeves. She holds a feather duster in

"COME IN."

her right hand, and in her left is a jar of
Royal Worcester. "Mary," Mrs. Edwards
says, severely, " where are we at ?"

Mary (*meekly*). " Boston, ma'am."

Mrs. Robert Edwards. " South Boston
or Boston proper ?"

Mary. " Boston proper, ma'am."

Mrs. Robert Edwards. " Then when I
say ' Who's there ?' don't say ' Me.' That
manner of speaking may do at New York,
Brooklyn, South Boston, or Congress, but
at Boston proper it is extremely gauche.
' I ' is the word."

Mary. " Yes, ma'am ; but you know,
ma'am, I don't pretend to be literary.
ma'am, and so these little points baffles I
very often." Mrs. Edwards sighs, and,
walking over to the window, looks out
upon the trolley - cars for ten minutes ;
then, picking up one of the pins from the
floor and putting it in a pink silk pin-
cushion which stands next to an alarm-
clock on the mantel-piece, a marble affair
with plain caryatids and a brass fender
around the hearth, she resumes her seat

before the sewing-machine, and threads a needle. Then—

Mrs. Robert Edwards. "Well, Mary, what do you want?"

Mary. "Please, Mrs. Edwards, the butcher is came, and he says they have some very fine perairie-chickens to-day."

Mrs. Robert Edwards. "We don't want any prairie-chickens. The prairies are so very vulgar. Tell him never to suggest such a thing again. Have we any potatoes in the house?"

Mary. "There's three left, ma'am, and two slices of cold roast beef."

Mrs. Robert Edwards. "Then tell him to bring five more potatoes, a steak, and— Was all the pickled salmon eaten?"

Mary. "All but the can, ma'am."

Mrs. Robert Edwards. "Well—Mr. Edwards is very fond of fish. Tell him to bring two boxes of sardines and a bottle of anchovy paste."

Mary. "Very well, Mrs. Edwards."

Mrs. Robert Edwards. "And — ah — Mary, tell him to bring some Brussels

64

MARY

sprouts for breakfast. What are you doing with that Worcester vase?"

Mary. "I was takin' it to cook, ma'am. Sure she broke the bean-pot this mornin', and she wanted somethin' to cook the beans in."

Mrs. Robert Edwards. "Oh, I see. Well, take good care of it, Mary. It's a rare piece. In fact, I think you'd better leave that here and remove the rubber plant from the jardinière, and let Nora cook the beans in that. Times are a little too hard to cook beans in Royal Worcester."

Mary. "Very well, ma'am." Mary goes out through the door. Mrs. Edwards resumes her sewing. Fifteen minutes elapse, interrupted only by the ticking of the alarm-clock and the occasional ringing of the bell on passing trolley-cars. "If it does rain," Mrs. Edwards says at last, with an anxious glance through the window, "I suppose Robert won't care about going to see the pantomime to-night. It will be too bad if we don't go, for this is

the last night of the season, and I've been
very anxious to renew my acquaintance
with 'Humpty Dumpty.' It is so very
dramatic, and I do so like dramatic
things. Even when they happen in my
own life I like dramatic things. I'll
never forget how I enjoyed the thrill
that came over me, even in my terror, that
night last winter when the trolley - car
broke down in front of this house; and
last summer, too, when the oar-lock broke
in our row - boat thirty - three feet from
shore; that was a situation that I enjoyed
in spite of its peril. How people can say
that life is humdrum, I can't see. Exciting things, real third - act situations, cli-
maxes I might even call them, are always
happening in my life, and yet some novel-
ists pretend that life is humdrum just to
excuse their books for being humdrum.
I'd just like to show these apostles of real-
ism the diary I could have kept if I had
wanted to. Beginning with the fall my
brother George had from the hay-wagon,
back in 1876, running down through my

THE OVERCOAT

first meeting with Robert, which was romantic enough—he paid my car-fare in from Brookline the day I lost my pocketbook — even to yesterday, when an entire stranger called me up on the telephone, my life has fairly bubbled with dramatic situations that would take the humdrum theory and utterly annihilate it." As Mrs. Edwards is speaking she is also sewing the button already alluded to on Mr. Edwards's coat as described. "There," taking the last stitch in the coat, "that's done, and now I can go and get ready for luncheon." She folds up the coat, glances at the clock, and goes out. A half-hour elapses. The silence is broken only by occasional noises from the street, the rattling of the wheels of a herdic over the pavement, the voices of newsboys, and an occasional strawberry - vender's cry. At the end of the half-hour the alarm-clock goes off and the curtain falls.

THE DREAMERS: A CLUB

The scene is laid in the drawing-room of Mr. and Mrs. Robert Edwards. Mrs. Edwards is discovered reading *Pendennis*, and seems in imminent danger of going to sleep over it. Mr. Edwards is stretched out upon the sofa, quite asleep, with *Ivanhoe* lying open upon his chest. Twenty-five minutes elapse, when the door-bell rings.

Mr. Edwards (drowsily). "Let me off at the next corner, conductor."

Mrs. Edwards. "Why, Robert — what nonsense you are talking !"

Mr. Edwards (rubbing his eyes and sitting up). "Eh ? What ? Nonsense ? I talk nonsense ? Really, my dear, that is a serious charge to bring against one of the leading characters in a magazine farce. Wit, perhaps, I may indulge in, but nonsense, never !"

Mrs. Edwards. "That is precisely what

70

EDWARDS REBELS

I complain about. The idea of a well-established personage like yourself lying off on a sofa in his own apartment and asking a conductor to let him off at the next corner! It's—"

Mr. Edwards. "I didn't do anything of the sort."

Mrs. Edwards. "You did, too, Robert Edwards. And I can prove it. If you will read back to the opening lines of this scene you will find that I have spoken the truth—unless you forgot your lines. If you admit that, I have nothing to say, but I will add that if you are going to forget lines that give the key-note of the whole situation, you've got no business in a farce. You'll make the whole thing fall flat some day, and then you will be discharged."

Mr. Edwards. "Well, I wish I might be discharged; I'm tired of the whole business. Anybody 'd take me for an idiot, the way I have to go on. Every bit of fun there is to be had in these farces is based upon some predicament into which

THE DREAMERS: A CLUB

my idiocy or yours gets me. Are we
idiots ? I ask you that. Are we ? You
may be, but, Mrs. Edwards, I am not. The
idea of my falling asleep over *Ivanhoe!*
Would I do that if I had my way ? Well,
I guess not ! Would I even dare to say
'I guess not' in a magazine farce ? Again,
I guess not. I'm going to write to the
editor this very night, and resign my situation. I want to be me. I don't want
to be what some author thinks I ought to
be. Do you know what I think ?"

Mrs. Edwards (*warningly*). "Take care,
Robert. Take care. You aren't employed
to think."

Mr. Edwards. "Precisely. That's what
makes me so immortally mad. The author
doesn't give me time to think. I could
think real thoughts if he'd let me, but
then ! The curtain wouldn't stay up half
a second if I did that ; and where would
the farce be ? The audience would go
home tired, because they wouldn't get
their nap if the curtain was down. It's
hard luck ; and as for me, I wouldn't keep

the position a minute if I could get anything else to do. Nobody 'd give me work,
now that I've been made out to be such
a confounded jackass. But let's talk of
other things."

Mrs. Edwards. "I'd love to, Robert—but we can't. There are no other
things in the farce. The Billises are
coming."

Mr. Edwards. "Hang the Billises!
Can't we ever have an evening to ourselves ?"

Mrs. Edwards. "How you do talk!
How can we ? There's got to be some
action in the farce, and it's the Billis
family that draws out our peculiarities."

Mr. Edwards. "Well, I'm going out,
and you can receive the Billises, and if it's
necessary for me to say anything to give
go to the play, you can say it. I make you
my proxy."

Mrs. Edwards. "It can't be done, Robert. They are here. The bell rang ten
minutes ago, and they ought to have got
in here five minutes since. You can't go

75

out without meeting them in the wings—
I mean the hallway."

Mr. Edwards. "Lost!"

Enter MR. *and* MRS. BILLIS.

Billis. "Ah, Edwards! Howdy do?
Knew you were home. Saw light in—"

Mrs. Billis. "Don't rattle on so, my
dear. Speak more slowly, or the farce will
be over before nine."

Billis. "I've got to say my lines, and
I'm going to say them my way. Ah,
Edwards! Howdy do? Knew you were
home. Saw light in window. Knew your
economical spirit. Said to myself must be
home, else why gas? He doesn't burn
gas when he's out. Wake up—"

Mr. Edwards. "I'm not asleep. Fact
is, I am going out."

Mrs. Billis. "Out?"

Mrs. Edwards. "Robert!"

Mr. Edwards. "That's what I said—
out. *O-u-t.*"

Billis. "Not bad idea. Go with you.
Where to?"

THE OVERCOAT

Mr. Edwards. "Anywhere — to find a tragedy and take part in it. I'm done farcing, my boy."

Billis (*slapping* Edwards *on back*). "Rah! my position exactly. I'm sick of it too. Come ahead. I know that fellow Whoy:—he'll take us in and give us a chance."

Mrs. Billis. "I've been afraid of this."

Mrs. Edwards. "Robert, consider your family."

Mr. Edwards. "I have; and if I'm to die respected and honored, if my family is to have any regard for my memory, I've got to get out of farcing. That's all. Did you sew the button on my overcoat?"

Mrs. Edwards. "I did. I'll go get it." She goes out. Mrs. Billis throws herself sobbing on sofa. Billis dances a jig. Forty minutes elapse, during which Billis's dance may be encored. Enter Mrs. Edwards, triumphantly, with overcoat.

Mrs. Edwards. "There's your overcoat."

Mr. Edwards. " But—but the button isn't sewed on. I can't go out in this."

Mrs. Edwards. " I knew it, Robert. I sewed the button on the wrong coat." Billis and Robert fall in a faint. Mrs. Billis rises and smiles, grasping Mrs. Edwards's hand fervently.

Mrs. Billis. " Noble woman !"

Mrs. Edwards. " Yes ; I've saved the farce."

Mrs. Billis. " You have. For, in spite of these—these strikers — these theatric Debses, you—you got in the point ! *The button was sewed on the wrong overcoat !"*

CURTAIN.

" When the farce was finished," said Mr. Parke, " and the applause which greeted the fall of the curtain had subsided, I dreamed also the following author's note : ' The elapses ' in this farce may seem rather long, but the reader must remember that it is the author's intention that his farce, if acted, should last

78

throughout a whole evening. If it were not for the elapses the acting time would be scarcely longer than twenty minutes, instead of two hours and a half."

"I mention this," Mr. Parke added, "not only in justification of myself, but also as a possible explanation of certain shortcomings in the work of the original master. Sometimes the action may seem to drag a trifle, but that is not the fault of the author, but of life itself. To be real one must be true, and truth is not to be governed by him who holds the pen."

Mr. Parke's explanation having been received in a proper and appreciative spirit by his fellow-Dreamers, Mr. Jones announced that Mr. Monty St. Vincent was the holder of the sixth ball, whereupon Mr. St. Vincent arose and delivered himself as follows :

V

THE SALVATION OF FINDLAYSON

*Being the story told by the holder of the sixth ball,
Mr. Monty St. Vincent.*

A DONKEY ENGINE, next to a Sopho-
more at a football match that is going his
way, is the noisiest thing man ever made,
and No. 4-11-44, who travelled first-class on
the American liner *New York,* was not inclined to let anybody forget the fact.
He held a commanding position on the
roof of the deck state-room No. 10, just
aft of the forecastle stringer No. 3, and
over the main jib-stay boom No. 6⅞, that
held the rudder-chains in place. All the
little Taffrails and Swashbucklers looked
up to him, and the Capstan loved him like
a brother, for he very often helped the

Capstan to bring the Anchor aboard, when otherwise that dissipated bit of iron would have staid out all night. The Port Tarpaulins insisted that the Donkey Engine was the greatest humorist that ever lived, although the Life Preservers hanging by the rail did not like him at all, because he once said they were Irish—"Cork all through," said he. Even the Rivets that held the Top Gallant Bilges together used to strain their eyes to see the points of the Donkey Engine's jokes, and the third Deputy-assistant Piston Rod, No. 683, in the hatchway stoke-hole, used to pound the cylinders almost to pieces trying to encore the Donkey Engine's comic songs.

The Main Mast used to say that the Donkey Engine was as bright as the Starboard Lights, and the Smoke Stack is said to have told the Safety Valve that he'd rather give up smoking than lose the constant flow of wit the Donkey Engine was always giving forth.

Findlayson discovered all this. After his Bridge had gone safely through that terrible ordeal when the Ganges rose and struck for higher tides, Findlayson collapsed. The Bridge— But that is another story. This is this one, and there is little profit in telling two stories at once, especially in a day when one can get the two stories printed separately in the several magazines for which one writes exclusively.

After the ordeal of the Kashi Bridge, Findlayson, as I have said, collapsed, and it is no wonder, as you will see for yourself when you read that other story. As the Main Girder of the Bridge itself wrote later to the Suspension Cables of the Brooklyn Bridge, "It's a wonder to me that the Sahib didn't have the *Bashi-bazouks* earlier in the game. He suffered a terrible strain that night."

To which the Cables of the Brooklyn Bridge wittily replied that while they sympathized with Findlayson, they didn't believe he really knew what strain was. "Wait until he has five lines of trolley-cars running over him all day and night.

That *is* a strain ! He'd be worse cut up than ever if he had that. And yet we thrive under it. After all, for solid health, it's better to be a Bridge than a Man. When are you coming across ?"

Now Findlayson might have collapsed a dozen times before the Government would have cared enough to give him the vacation he needed. Not that Government is callous, like an elephant, but because it is conducted, as a witty Cobra once remarked in the jungle as he fascinated a Tigress, by a lot of Red Tapirs. Findlayson put in an application for a six months' vacation, but by the time the necessary consent had reached him the six months were up. Everybody remembers the tale of Dorkins of the Welsh Fusileers and his appointment to the Department of the Poloese, how his term of office was to be six years, and how by the time his credentials reached him his term of office had expired. So with Findlayson. On the very date of the expiration of his desired leave he received permission to go, and of course could not then do so, because it was too late. Fortunately for Findlayson, however, the Viceroy himself happened to be passing through, and Findlayson entertained him at a luncheon on the Bridge. By some curious mistake, when the nuts and raisins were passed, Findlayson had provided a plateful of steel nuts, designed to hold rivets in place, instead of the usual assortment of almonds and *hiki-ree.*

"This man needs a rest," said the Viceroy, as he broke his front tooth trying to crack one of the steel nuts, and he immediately extended Findlayson's leave to twenty years without pay, for which Findlayson was very grateful.

"What is the matter with the man?" asked the Viceroy, as he drove to the station with the practising Jinrikshaw of the place.

"It's my professional opinion," replied the Jinrikshaw, "that the Sahib has a bad attack of melancholia. He hasn't laughed for six months. If we could

THE VICEROY EXAMINES HIS RUINED SMILE

only get him to laugh, I think he'd recover."

"Then it was not in a jocular spirit that he ruined my teeth with those nuts?" demanded the Viceroy, taking a small mirror out of his pocket and gazing ruefully on his ruined smile.

"No, your most Excellent Excellency," replied the Jinrikshaw. "The fact that he ate five of them himself shows that it was an error, not a jest."

It was thus that Findlayson got his vacation, and even to this day the Kaskalooloo folk are laughing over his error more heartily than they ever laughed over a joke.

A month after leaving his post Findlayson reached London, where he was placed under the care of the most famous physicians. They did everything they could to make him laugh, without success. *Punch* was furnished, and he read it through day after day, and burst into hysterical weeping. They took him to the theatres, and he never even smiled.

They secured a front seat in the House of
Commons for him during important de-
bates, and he merely sobbed. They took
him to the Army and Navy Stores, and he
shivered with fear. Even Beerbohm Tree
as Lady Macbeth, or whatever rôle it was
he was playing at the time, failed to coax
the old - time dimple to his cheek. His
friends began to whisper among themselves that "old Findlayson was done
for," when Berkeley Hauksbee, who had
been with him in the Soudan, suggested a
voyage to the United States.

"He'll see enough there to laugh at,
or I'm an unshod, unbroken, saw-backed,
shark-eating skate !" he asserted, and as a
last resource Findlayson was packed, bag
and baggage, aboard the liner *New York.*

The first three days out Findlayson was
dead to the world. He lay like a fallen
log in the primeval forest. Stewards
were of no avail. Even the repeated calls
of the doctor, whose apprehensions were
aroused, could not restore him to life.

"They'll be sewin' him up in a jute
88

THEY GAVE HIM *PUNCH*

bag and droppin' him overboard if he doesn't come to by to-morrow," observed the Water Bottle to the Soap Dish, with a sympathetic glance at the prostrate Findlayson.

"He'll be seasicker than ever if they do," returned the Soap Dish. "It's a long swim from here to Sandy Hook."

But Findlayson came to in time to avert the catastrophe, and took several turns up and down the deck. He played horse-billiards with an English curate, but showed no sign of interest or amusement even at the curious aspect of the ladies who lay inert in the steamer chairs ranged along the deck.

"I'm afraid it's hopeless," said Peroo, his valet, shaking his head sadly. "Unless I take him in hand myself." And Peroo was seized with an idea.

"I'll do it!" he cried.

He approached Findlayson.

"The Sahib will not laugh," he said. "He will not smile even. He has not snickered all day. Take these, then.

They're straight opium, but there's fun in them."

He took a small zinc bait-box from his fishing-kit and handed it to Findlayson, who, on opening it, found a dozen or more brown pellets. Hastily swallowing six of them, the sick man turned over in his bunk and tried to go to sleep, while Peroo went into the smoking-room for a game of *Pok-Kah* with a party of *Drummerz* who were crossing to America.

A soft yellow haze suffused the state-room, and Findlayson, nervously starting to his feet to see what had caused it, was surprised to find himself confronted by a grinning row of Technicalities ranged in a line upon the sofa under the port, while seated upon his steamer trunk was the Donkey Engine 4-11-44.

" Well, here we are," said the Deck Beam, addressing the Donkey Engine. " What are we here for ?"

" That's it," said the Capstan. " We've left our places at your command. Now, why ?"

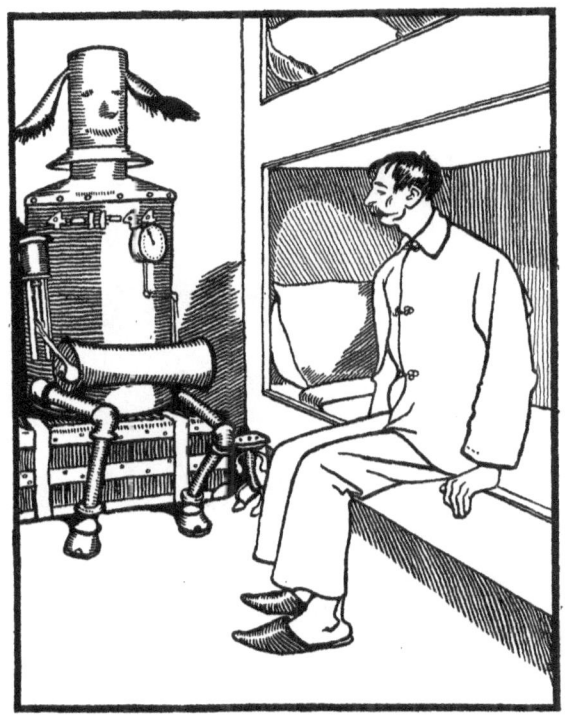

THE DONKEY ENGINE CALLS ON FINDLAYSON

"I wanted you to meet my friend
Findlayson," said the Donkey Engine.
" He's a good fellow. Findlayson, let me
present you to my associates—Mr. Capstan, Mr. Findlayson. And that gentleman over in the corner, Mr. Findlayson,
is the Starboard Upper Deck Stringer.
Rivet, come over here and meet Mr.
Findlayson. The Davits will be here in
a minute, and the Centrifugal Bilge Pump
will drop in later."

" I'm glad to meet you all," said Findlayson, rather dazed.

" Thought you would be," returned the
Donkey Engine. " That's why I asked
them to come up."

" Do you mind if I smoke in here ?"
said the Funnel.

" Not a bit," said Findlayson, solemn-
ly. " Let me offer you a cigar."

The party roared at this.

" He doesn't smoke cigars, Fin, old
boy," said the Donkey Engine. " Offer
him a ton of coal Perfectos or a basket of
kindling Invincibles and he'll take you

up. Old Funnel makes a cigarette of a cord of pine logs, you know."

"I should think so much smoking would be bad for your nerves," suggested Findlayson.

"'Ain't got any," said the Funnel. "I'm only a Flue, you know. Every once in a while I do get a sooty feeling inside, but beyond that I don't suffer at all."

"Where's the Keel ?" asked the Thrust Block, taking off one of his six collars, which hurt his neck.

"He can't come up to-night," said the Donkey Engine, with a sly wink at Findlayson, who, however, failed to respond. "The Hold is feeling a little rocky, and the Keel's got to stay down and steady him."

Findlayson looked blankly at the Donkey Engine. As an Englishman in a nervously disordered state, he did not seem quite able to appreciate the Donkey Engine's joke. The latter sighed, shook his cylinder a trifle, and began again.

"Hear about the Bow Anchor's row with the Captain?" he asked the Garboard Strake.

"No," replied the Strake. "Wouldn't he bow?"

"He'd bow all right," said the Donkey Engine, "but he wouldn't ank. Result is he's been put in chains."

"Serves him right," said the Bilge Stringer, filling his pipe with Findlayson's tooth-powder. "Serves him right. He ought to be chucked overboard."

"True," said the Donkey Engine. "An anchor can't be made to ank unless you chuck him overboard."

The company roared at this, but Findlayson never cracked a smile.

"That is very true," he said. "In fact, how could an anchor ank, as you put it, without being lowered into the sea?"

"It's a bad case," observed Bulwark Plate, in a whisper, to the Upper Deck Plank.

"It floors me," said the Plank. "I

G   97

don't think he'd laugh if his uncle died and left him a million."

"Shut up," said the Donkey Engine. "We've got to do it or bust. Let's try again."

Then he added, aloud,

"Say, Technicalities, did you ever hear that riddle of the Starboard Coal Bunker's ?"

The company properly had not.

"Well, the Starboard Coal Bunker got it off at Lady Airshaft's last reception at Binks's Ship-yard : ' What's the difference between a man-o'-war going through the Suez Canal under tow of a tug-boat and a boiler with a capacity of 6000 tons of steam loaded to 7000 tons, with no safety-valve, in charge of an engineer who has a certificate from Bellevue Hospital showing that he is a good ambulance-driver, but supports a widowed mother and seven uncles upon no income to speak of, all of which is invested in Spanish fours, bought on a margin of two per cent. in a Wall Street bucket-shop conducted by two

98

professional card-players from Honolulu under indictment at San Francisco for arson ?'"

"Tutt!" said the Rudder. "What a chestnut! I was brought up on riddles of that kind. *They can't climb a tree.*"

"Nope," said the Donkey Engine. "That's not the answer."

"You don't know it yourself," suggested the Funnel.

"Nope," said the Donkey Engine.

"Well, what the deuce is the answer?" said Findlayson, irritably.

"Give it up—the rest of you?" cried the Donkey Engine.

"We do," they roared in chorus.

"I'm surprised at you," said the Donkey Engine. "It's very simple indeed. The man-o'-war going through the Suez Canal under tow of a tug-boat has a pull —and the other hasn't, don't you know— eh ?"

Findlayson scratched his forehead.

"I don't see—" he began.

"There is no reason why you should.

You're not feeling well," interrupted the Donkey Engine, " but it's a good riddle— eh ?"

"Quite so," said Findlayson.

"It's long, anyhow," said the Screw.

"Which we can't say for to-day's run— only 867 miles ?" suggested the Donkey Engine, interrogatively.

"It's long enough," growled the Screw.

"It certainly is, if it is reckoned in minutes," retorted the Donkey Engine. "I never knew such a long day."

And so they continued in an honest and technical effort to restore Findlayson. But he wouldn't laugh, and finally the Screw and the Centrifugal Bilge Pump and the Stringers and the other well-meaning Technicalities rose up to leave. Day was approaching, and all were needed at their various posts.

"Good-night—or good-morning, Findlayson," said the Donkey Engine. "We've had a very pleasant night. I am only sorry, however, we cannot make you laugh."

"I never laugh," said Findlayson.

"But tell me, old chap, are you really human? You talk as if you were."

"No," returned the Donkey Engine, sadly. "I am neither fish, flesh, nor fowl. I'm a *bivalve—a cockney bivalve*," he added.

"Oh," replied Findlayson, with a gesture of deprecation, "you are not a clam !"

"No," the Donkey Engine replied, as with a sudden inspiration ; "but I'm a hoister."

And Findlayson burst into a paroxysm of mirth—it must be remembered that he was English—the like of which the good old liner never heard before.

And later, when Peroo returned, having won at *Pok-Kah* with the *Drummerz*, he found his master sleeping like the veriest child.

Findlayson was saved.

VI

MONTY ST. VINCENT had no sooner
seated himself after telling the interesting
tale of the Salvation of Findlayson, when
Billy Jones, of the *Oracle*, rose up and
stated that Mr. Harry Snobbe, as the
holder of the seventh ball, would unfold
the truly marvellous story that had come
to him after the first dinner of the
Dreamers.

"Mr. Snobbe requests all persons having nerves to be unstrung to unstring
them now. His tale, he tells me, is one
of intense gloom ; but how intense the
gloom may be, I know not. I will leave it
to him to show. Gentlemen, Mr. Snobbe."

A TALE OF GLOOM

Mr. Snobbe took the floor, and after a
few preliminary remarks, read as follows:

THE GLOOMSTER

A TALE OF THE ISLE OF MAN

Old Gloomster Goodheart, of Ballyhack,
left the Palace of the Bishop of Man
broken - hearted. The Bishop had summoned him a week previous to show cause
why he should not be removed from his
office of Gloomster, a position that had
been held by members of his family for
ten generations, aye, since the days of
that ancient founder of the family, Cronky
Gudehart, of whom tradition states that
his mere presence at a wedding turned
the marriage feast into a seeming funeral
ceremony, making men and women weep,
and on two occasions driving the bride to
suicide and the groom into the Church.
Indeed, Cronky Gudehart was himself the
first to occupy the office of Gloomster.
The office was created for his especial benefit, as you will see, for it was the mere

fact that the two grooms bereft at the altar sought out the consolation of the monastery that called the attention of the ecclesiastical authorities to the desirability of establishing such a functionary. The two grooms were men of wealth, and, had it not been for Cronky Gudehart's malign influence, neither they nor their wealth would have passed into the control of the Church, a fact which Ramsay Ballawhaine, then Bishop of Man, was quick to note and act upon.

"The gloomier the world," said he, "the more transcendently bright will Heaven seem; and if we can make Heaven seem bright, the Church will be able to declare dividends. Let us spread misery and sorrow. Let us destroy the sunshine of life that so gilds with glory the flesh and the devil. Let all that is worldly be made to appear mean and vile and sordid."

"But how?" Ramsay Ballawhaine was asked. "That is a hard thing to do."

"For some 'twill doubtless so appear, but I have a plan," the Bishop had an-

104

swered. "We have here living, not far
from Jellimacksquizzle, the veriest spoil-
sport in the person of Cronky Gudehart.
He has a face that would change the
August beauties of a sylvan forest into a
bleak scene of wintry devastation. I am
told that when Cronky Gudehart gazes
upon a rose it withers, and children passing him in the highways run shrieking to
their mothers, as though escaping from
the bogie man of Caine Hall—which castle, as you know, has latterly been haunted
by horrors that surpass the imagination.
His voice is like the strident cry of doom.
Hearing his footsteps, strong men quail
and women swoon; and I am told that,
dressed as Santa Claus, on last Christmas
eve he waked up his sixteen children, and
with a hickory stick belabored one and all
until they said that mercy was all they
wanted for their Yule-tide gifts."

"'Tis true," said the assistant vicar.
"'Tis very true; and I happen to know,
through my own ministrations, that when
a beggar-woman from Sodor applied to

Cronky Gudehart for relief from the sorrows of the world, he gave her a bottle of carbolic acid, saying that therein lay the cure of all her woes. But what of Cronky and your scheme ?"

"Let us establish the office of Gloomster," returned the Bishop. "Set apart Nightmare Abbey as his official residence, and pay him a salary to go about among the people spreading grief and woe among them until they fly in desperation to us who alone can console."

"It's out of sight!" ejaculated the assistant vicar, "and Cronky's just the man for the place."

It was thus that the office of Gloomster was instituted. As will be seen, the duties of the Gloomster were simple. He was given liberty of entrance to all joyous functions in the life of the Isle of Man, social or otherwise, and his duties were to ruin pleasure wherever he might find it. Cronky Gudehart was installed in the office, and Nightmare Abbey was set apart as his official residence. He attended all weddings, and spoiled them in so far as he was able. It was his custom, when the vicar asked if there was any just reason why these two should not be joined together in holy wedlock, to rise up and say that, while he had no evidence at hand, he had no doubt there was just cause in great plenty, and to suggest that the ceremony should be put off a week or ten days while he and his assistants looked into the past records of the principals. At funerals he took the other tack, and laughed joyously at every manifestation of grief. At hangings he would appear, and dilate humorously upon the horrid features thereof; and at afternoon teas he would appear clad in black garments from head to foot, and exhort all present to beware of the future, and to give up the hollowness and vanities of tea and macaroons.

Results were not long in their manifestation. In place of open marriage the young people of the isle, to escape the malignant persecution of the Gloomster, took up the habit of elopement, and as elopements always end in sorrow and regret, the monasteries and nunneries waxed great in the land. To avoid funerals, at which the Gloomster's wit was so fearsome a thing, the sick or the maimed and the halt fled out into the open sea and drowned themselves, and all sociability save that which came from book sales and cake auctions — in their very nature destructive of a love of life — faded out of the land.

"Cronky Gudehart was an ideal Gloomster," said the Bishop of Man, with a sigh, when that worthy spoil-sport, having gone to Africa for a vacation, was eaten by cannibals. "We shall not look upon his like again."

"I've no doubt he disagreed with the cannibals," sobbed the vicar, as he thought over the virtues of the deceased.

"None who ate him could escape appendicitis," commented the Bishop, wiping a tear from his eye; "and, thank Heaven, the operation for that has yet to be invented. Those cannibals have

108

THE END OF THE GLOOMSTER

been taken by this time from their wicked life."

So it had gone on for ten generations. Cronky had been succeeded by his son and by his son's son, and so on. To be Gloomster of the Isle of Man had by habit become the prerogative of the Gudehart family until the present, when Christian Goodheart found himself summoned before the Bishop to show cause why he should not be removed. Hitherto the Gloomster had given satisfaction. It would be hard to point to one of them— unless we except Eric Goodheart, the one who changed the name from Gudehart to Goodheart—who had not filled the island with that kind of sorrow that makes life seem hardly worth living. Eric Goodheart had once caught his father, "Bully Gudehart," as he was called, in a moment of forgetfulness, doing a kindly act to a beggar at the door. A wanderer had appeared at the door of Nightmare Abbey in a starving condition, and Eric had surprised the Gloomster in the very act of

111

giving the beggar a piece of apple-pie. The father found himself suddenly confronted by the round, staring eyes of his son, and he was frightened. If it were ever known that the Gloomster had done a kindly thing for anybody, he might be removed, and Bully Gudehart recognized the fact.

"Come here!" he cried brutally, to Eric, as the beggar marched away munching hungrily on the pie. "Come here, you brat! Do you hear? Come *here!*" The boy was coming all the while. "You saw?"

"Yes, your Honor," he replied, "I saw. The man said he was nearly dead with hunger, and you gave him food."

"No," roared the Gloomster, full of fear, for he knew how small boys prattle, "I did not give him food! *I gave him pie!*"

"All right, your Majesty," the boy answered. "You gave him pie. And I see now why they call you Bully. For pie is bully, and nothing less."

"My son," the Gloomster responded, seizing a trunk-strap and whacking the lad with it forcefully, "you don't under-

112

stand. Do you know why I fed that man?"

"Because he was dying of hunger," replied the lad, ruefully, rubbing his back where the trunk-strap had hit him.

"Precisely," said the Gloomster. "If I hadn't given him that pie he'd have died on the premises, and I can't afford the expense of having a tramp die here. As it is, he will enjoy a lingering death. *That was one of your mother's pies.*"

Eric ran sobbing to his room, but in his heart he believed that he had detected his father in a kindly act, and conceived that a Gloomster might occasionally relax. Nevertheless, when he succeeded to the office he was stern and unrelenting, in spite of the fact that occasionally there was to be detected in his eye a glance of geniality. This was doubtless due to the fact that from the time of his intrusion upon his father's moment of weakness he was soundly thrashed every morning before breakfast, and spanked before retiring at night, as a preliminary to his prayers.

But Christian Goodheart, the present incumbent, had not given satisfaction, and his Bishop had summoned him to show cause why he should not be removed, and, as we have seen, the Gloomster had gone away broken-hearted. Shortly after having arrived at Nightmare Abbey he was greeted by his wife.

" Well, Christian," she said, " what did the Bishop say ?"

" He wants my resignation," sighed Christian. " He says I have shown myself unworthy, and I fear he has evidence."

" Evidence ? Against you, my husband, the most disagreeable man in the isle ?" cried his wife, fondly.

" Yes," sighed Christian. " Do you remember, you old termagant, how, forgetting myself and my position, last Tuesday I laughed when Peter Skelly told us what his baby said to his nurse ?"

" I do, Christian," the good woman answered. " You laughed heartily, and I warned you to be careful. It is not the

114

Gloomster's place to laugh, and I feared it might reach the Bishop's ears."

"It has done so," sighed Christian, shaking his head sadly and wringing his hands in his agony. "It has reached the Bishop's ears. Little Glory Grouse was passing by the door at the moment and saw me. Astonished, the child ran home and told her mother. 'Mommer!' she cried, 'I have seen the Gloomster laugh! I have seen the Gloomster laugh!' The child was cross-questioned, but stuck to her story until Mrs. Grouse was convinced, and told her neighbors, and these neighbors told other neighbors, until the story came to the ears of Canon Cashman, by whom it was conveyed to the Bishop himself."

"What a little gossip that Glory Grouse is! She'll come to a bad end, mark my words!" cried Mrs. Goodheart, angrily. "She'll have her honored father's name on the circus posters yet."

"Do not blame the child," said Christian, sadly. "She was right. Who had

ever seen a Gloomster smile before ? As
well expect a ray of sunshine or a glimpse
of humor in a Manx novel—"

" But the Bishop is not going to remove
you for one false step, is he, Christian ?
He cannot do that, can he ?" pleaded the
woman.

"That is what I asked him ?" Christian
answered. " And he handed me a type-
written memorandum of what he called
my record. It seems that for six months
they have been spying upon me. Read it
for yourself."

Mrs. Goodheart took the paper and read,
with trembling hands :

" ' January 1, 1898—wished Peggy Meguire a happy New Year.' Did you really, Christian ?"

"I don't remember doing so," sighed the
Gloomster. "If I did, it must have been
in sarcasm, for I hate Peggy Meguire, and
I am sure I wish her nothing of the sort.
I told the Bishop so, but all he would say
was, ' Read on.' "

" ' February 23, 1898,' " Mrs. Good-

WISHED HER A HAPPY NEW-YEAR

heart continued, reading from the paper
—"'took off his coat and wrapped it about
the shivering form of a freezing woman.'

"How very imprudent of you, Christian !" said his wife.

"But the Bishop didn't know the circumstances," said Christian. " It was the
subtlest kind of deviltry, not humanity,
that prompted the act. If I hadn't given
her my coat, the old lady would have
frozen to death and been soon out of her
misery. As it was, my wet coat saved her
from an immediate surcease of sorrow,
and, as I had foreseen, gave her muscular
rheumatism of the most painful sort,
from which she has suffered ever since."

" You should have explained to the
Bishop."

" I did."

" And what did he say ?"

" He said my methods were too damned
artistic."

"What ?" cried Mrs. Goodheart. " The
Bishop ?"

" Oh, well," said Christian, " words to

that effect. He doesn't appreciate the subtleties of gloom distinction. What he looks for is sheer brutality. Might as well employ an out-and-out desperado for the work. I like to infuse a little art into my work. I've tried to bring Gloomsterism up to the level of an art, a science. Slapping a man in the face doesn't make him gloomy; it makes him mad. But subtlely infusing woe into his daily life, so that he doesn't know whence all his trouble comes—ah! that is the perfect flower of the Gloomster's work!"

"H'm!" said Mrs. Goodheart. "That's well enough, Christian. If you are rich enough to consume your own product with profit, it's all right to be artistic; but if you are dependent on a salary, don't forget your consumer. What else have they against you?"

"Read on, woman," said the Gloomster.

"'April 1, 1898,'" the lady read. "'Gave a half-crown to a starving beggar.'"

A TALE OF GLOOM

" That was another highly artistic act,"
said Christian. " I told the Bishop that
I had given the coin to the beggar knowing it to be counterfeit, and hoping that
he would be arrested for trying to pass it.
The Bishop cut me short by saying that
my hope had not been fulfilled. It seems
that that ass of a beggar bought some
food with the half-crown, and the grocer
who sold him the food put the counterfeit
half-crown in the contribution-box the
next Sunday, and the Church was stuck.
That's what I call hard luck."

" Oh, well," returned Mrs. Goodheart.
putting the paper down in despair.
" There's no need to read further. That
alone is sufficient to cause your downfall.
When do you resign ?"

" At once," sighed Christian. " In fact,
the Bishop had already written my resignation—which I signed."

" And the land is without a Gloomster
for the first time in five hundred years ?"
demanded Mrs. Goodheart.

" No," said Christian, the tears coursing

down his nose. "The place is filled already, and by one who knows gloom only theoretically—a mere summer resident of the Isle of Man. In short, a famous London author has succeeded me."

"His name!" cried Mrs. Goodheart.

.   .   .   .

"Just then," said Snobbe, "I awoke, and did not catch the author's name. It is a curious thing about dreams that just when you get to the crucial point you wake up."

"I wonder who the deuce the chap could have been?" murmured the other diners. "Has any London author with a residence on the Isle of Man ever shown any acquaintance with gloom?"

"I don't know for sure," said Billy Jones. "But my impression is that it must be the editor of *Punch*. What I am uncertain about is his residence on the Isle of Man. Otherwise I think he fills the bill."

VII

THE DREAMERS DISCUSS A MAGAZINE POEM

THE pathetic tale of the Gloomster having been told and discussed, it turned out that Haarlem Bridge was the holder of the next ball in the sequence, the eighth. Haarley had been looking rather nervous all the evening, and two or three times he manifested some desire to withdraw from the scene. By order of the chairman, however, the precaution had been taken to lock all the doors, so that none of the Dreamers should escape, and, consequently, when the evil hour arrived, Haarley was perforce on hand.

He rose up reluctantly, and, taking a single page of manuscript from his pocket, after a few preliminary remarks that were no more nor less coherent than the aver-

age after-dinner speech, read the following lines, which he termed a magazine
poem :

" O argent-browed Sarcophagus,
    That looms so through the ethered trees,
 Why dost thou seem to those of us
    Who drink the poisoned chalice on our knees
 So distant and so empyrean,
    So dour yet full of mystery ?
 Hast thou the oracle as yet unseen
    To guide thy fell misogyny ?

"Nay, let the spirit of the age
    With all its mystic beauty stand
 Translucent ever, aye, in spite the rage
    Of Cossack and of Samarcand !
 Thou art enough for any soul's desire !
 Thou hast the beauty of cerulean fire !
 But we who grovel on the damask earth
 Are we despoilt of thy exigeant mirth ?

" Canst listen to a prayer, Sarcophagus ?
 Indeed O art thou there, Sarcophagus ?
 What time the Philistine denies,
 What time the raucous cynic cries,
 Avaunt, yet spare ! Let this thy motto be,
 With thy thesaurian verbosity.
 Nor think that I, a caterpillian worm,
 Before thy glance should ever honk or squirm.

"'O ARGENT-BROWED SARCOPHAGUS'"

A MAGAZINE POEM

"'Tis but the stern condition of the poor
That panting brings me pottering at thy door,
To breathe of love and argent charity
For thee, for thee, iguanodonic thee!"

"That's an excellent specimen of magazine poetry," said Billy Jones. "But I
observe, Haarley, that you haven't given it
a title. Perhaps if you gave it a title we
might get at the mystery of its meaning.
A title is a sort of Baedeker to the general run of magazine poems."

Haarlem grew rather red of counte-
nance as he answered, "Well, I didn't exactly like to give it the title I dreamed; it
didn't seem to shed quite as much light
on the subject as a title should."

"Still, it may help," said Huddy Rivers.
"I read a poem in a magazine the other
day on 'Mystery.' And if it hadn't had a
title I'd never have understood it. It ran
this way:

"Life, what art thou? Whence springest thou?
The past, the future, or the now?
Whence comes thy lowering lunacy?
Whence comes thy mizzling mystery?

127

THE DREAMERS: A CLUB

Hast thou a form, a shape, a lineament ?
Hast thou a single seraph-eyed medicament
To ease our sorrow and our twitching woe ?
Hast thou one laudable Alsatian glow
To compensate, commensurate, and condign
For all these dastard, sleekish qualms of mine ?
Hast thou indeed an abject agate plot
To show that what exists is really not ?
Or art thou just content to sit and say
Life's but a specious, coral roundelay ?"

" I committed the thing to memory because it struck me as being a good thing
to remember — it was so full of good
phrases. 'Twitching woe,' for instance,
and 'sleekish qualms,' " he continued.

" Quaking qualms would have been better," put in Tenafly Paterson, who judged
poetry from an alliterative point of
view.

"Nevertheless, I liked sleekish qualms,"
retorted Huddy. "Quaking qualms might
be more alliterative, but sleekish qualms
is *less* commonplace."

" No doubt," said Tenafly. " I never
had 'em myself, so I'll take your word for

128

it. But what do you make out of 'coral roundelay'?"

"Nothing at all," said Huddy. "I don't bother my head about 'coral roundelay' or 'seraph - eyed medicament.' I haven't wasted an atom of my gray matter on 'lowering lunacy' or 'agate plot' or 'mizzling mystery.' And all because the poet gave his poem a title. He called the thing 'Mystery,' and when I had read it over half a dozen times I concluded that he was right; and if the thing remained a mystery to the author, I don't see why a reader should expect ever to be able to understand it."

"Very logical conclusion, Huddy," said Billy Jones, approvingly. "If a poet chooses a name for his poem, you may make up your mind that there is good reason for it, and certainly the verses you have recited about the 'coral roundelay' are properly designated."

"Well, I'd like to have the title of that yard of rhyme Haarlem Bridge just recited," put in Dobbs Ferry, scratching his

I   129

head in bewilderment. "It strikes me as being quite as mysterious as Huddy's. What the deuce can a man mean by referring to an 'auburn-haired Sarcophagus'?"

"It wasn't auburn - haired," expostulated Haarlem. "It was argent-browed."

"Old Sarcophagus had nickel - plated eyebrows, Dobby," cried Tom Snobbe, forgetting himself for a moment.

"Well, who the dickens was old Sarcophagus?" queried Dobby, unappeased.

"He was one of the Egyptian kings, my dear boy," vouchsafed Billy Jones, exploding internally with mirth. "You've heard of Augustus Cæsar, haven't you?"

"Yes," said Dobby.

"Well," explained Billy Jones, "Sarcophagus occupied the same relation to the Egyptians that Augustus did to the Romans—in fact, the irreverent used to call him Sarcophagustus, instead of Sarcophagus, which was his real name. This poem of Haarley's is manifestly addressed to him."

" SARCOPHAGUSTUS "

A MAGAZINE POEM

"Did he have nickel-plated eyebrows?" asked Bedfork Parke, satirically.

"No," said Billy Jones. "As I remember the story of Sarcophagus as I read of him in college, he was a very pallid sort of a potentate—his forehead was white as marble. So they called him the Argent-browed Sarcophagus."

"It's a good thing for us we have Billy Jones with us to tell us all these things," whispered Tom Snobbe to his brother Dick.

"You bet your life," said Dick. "There's nothing, after all, like a classical education. I wish I'd known it while I was getting mine."

"What's 'fell misogyny'?" asked Tenafly Paterson, who seemed to be somewhat enamoured of the phrase. "Didn't old Sarcophagus care for chemistry?"

"Chemistry?" demanded the chairman.

"That's what I said," said Tenny. "Isn't misogyny a chemical compound of metal and gas?"

Tenny had been to the School of Mines

for two weeks, and had retired because he didn't care for mathematics and the table at the college restaurant wasn't good.

"I fancy you are thinking of heterophemy, which is an infusion of unorthodox gases into a solution of vocabulary particles," suggested Billy Jones, grasping his sides madly to keep them from shaking.

"Oh yes, ' said Tenny, "of course. I remember now." Then he laughed somewhat, and added, "I always get misogyny and heterophemy mixed."

"Who wouldn't ?" cried Harry Snobbe. "I do myself ! There's no chance to talk about either where I live," he added. "Half the people don't know what they mean. They're not very anthropological up my way."

"What's a Samarcand ?" asked Tenafly, again. "Haarley's poem speaks of Cossack and of Samarcand. Of course we all know that a Cossack is a garment worn by the Russian peasants, but I never heard of a Samarcand."

"It's a thing to put about your neck,"
134

said Dick Snobbe. "They wear 'em in winter out in Siberia. I looked it up some years ago "

"Let's take up 'cerulean fire,'" said Bedford Parke, Tenafly appearing to be satisfied with Snobbe's explanation.

"What's 'cerulean fire'?"

"Blue ruin," said Huddy.

"And 'damask earth'?" said Bedford.

"Easy," cried Huddy. "Even I can understand that. Did you never hear, Beddy, of painting a town red? That's damask earth in a small way. If you can paint a town red with your limited resources, what couldn't a god do with a godlike credit? As I understand the poem, old Sarcophagus comes down out of the cerulean fire, and goes in for a little damask earth. That's why the poet later says :

> "'Canst listen to a prayer, Sarcophagus ?
> Indeed O art thou there, Sarcophagus ?'

He wanted to pray to him, but didn't know if he'd got back from damask earth yet."

135

"You're a perfect wonder, Huddy," said Billy Jones. "As a thought-detector you are a beauty. I believe you'd succeed if you opened up a literary bureau somewhere and devoted your time to explaining Browning and Meredith and others to a mystified public."

"'Tis an excellent idea," said Tom Snobbe. "I'd really rejoice to see certain modern British masterpieces translated into English, and, with headquarters in Boston, the institution ought to flourish. Do worms honk?"

"I never heard of any doing so," replied the chairman, "but in these days it is hardly safe to say that anything is impossible. If you have watched the development of the circus in the last five years— I mean the real circus, not the literary— you must have observed what an advance intellectually has been made by the various members of the animal kingdom. Elephants have been taught to sit at table and dine like civilized beings on things that aren't good for them ; pigs have been

136

MR. BILLY JONES

educated so that, instead of evincing none
but the more domestic virtues and stay-
ing contentedly at home, they now play
poker with the sangfroid of a man about
town; while the seal, a creature hitherto
considered useful only in the production
of sacques for our wives, and ear-tabs for
our children, and mittens for our hired
men, are now branching out as rivals to
the college glee clubs, singing songs, playing banjoes, and raising thunder generally. Therefore it need surprise no one
if a worm should learn to honk as high
as any goose that ever honked. Anyhow,
you can't criticise a poet for anything of
that kind. His license permits him to
take any liberties he may see fit with ex-
isting conditions."

"All of which," observed Dick Snobbe,
"is wandering from the original point of
discussion. What is the meaning of Haarley's poem? I can't see that as yet we
have reached a definite understanding on
that point."

"Well, I must confess," said Jones,

"that I can't understand it myself; but I never could understand magazine poetry, so that doesn't prove anything. I'm only a newspaper man."

"Let's have the title, Haarley," cried Tenafly Paterson. "Was it called 'Life,' or 'Nerve Cells,' or what?"

For a second Bridge's cheeks grew red.

"Oh, well, if you must have it," he said, desperately, "here it is. It was called, 'A Thought on Hearing, While Visiting Gibraltar in June, 1898, that the War Department at Washington Had Failed to Send Derricks to Cuba, Thereby Delaying the Landing of General Shafter Three Days and Giving Comfort to the Enemy.'"

"Great Scott!" roared Dick Snobbe. "What a title!"

"It is excellent," said Billy Jones. "I now understand the intent of the poem."

"Which was— ?" asked Rivers.

"To supply a real hiatus in latter-day letters," Jones replied; "to give the public a war poem that would make them think, which is what a true war poem should do. Who has the ninth ball ?"

" I am the unfortunate holder of that," said Greenwich Place. " I'd just been reading Anthony Hope and Mr. Dooley. The result is a composite, which I will read."

" What do you call it, Mr. Place ?" asked the stenographer.

" Well, I don't know," replied Greenwich. " I guess 'A Dooley Dialogue' about describes it."

VIII

DOLLY VISITS CHICAGO

*Being the substance of a Dooley dialogue dreamed
by Greenwich Place, Esq.*

"I MUST see him," said Dolly, rising
suddenly from her chair and walking to
the window. "I really must, you know."

"Who?" I asked, rousing myself from
the lethargy into which my morning paper had thrust me. It was not grammatical of me—I was somewhat under the influence of newspaper English—but Dolly
is quick to understand. "Must see who?"
I continued.

"Who indeed?" cried Dolly, gazing at
me in mock surprise. "How stupid of
you! If I went to Rome and said I must
see him, you'd know I must mean the

142

Pope ; if I went to Berlin and said I must
see it, you'd know I meant the Emperor.
Therefore, when I come to Chicago and
say that I must see him, you ought to be
able to guess that I mean—"

"Mr. Dooley ?" I ventured, at a guess.

"Good for you !" cried Dolly, clapping
her hands together joyously ; and then
she hummed bewitchingly, "The Boy
Guessed Right the Very First Time," until I begged her to desist. When Dolly
claps her hands and hums, she becomes
a vision of loveliness that would give
the most confirmed misogynist palpita-
tion of the heart, and I had no wish to
die.

"Do you suppose I could call upon
him without being thought too unconventional ?" she blurted out in a moment.

"You can do anything," said I, admir-
ingly. "That is, with me to help," I added, for I should be sorry if Dolly were to
grow conceited. "Perhaps it would be
better to have Mr. Dooley call upon you.
Suppose you send him your card, and put

'at home' on it? I fancy that would fetch him."

"Happy thought!" said Dolly. "Only I haven't one. In the excitement of our elopement I forgot to get any. Suppose I write my name on a blank card and send it?"

"Excellent," said I.

And so it happened; the morning's mail took out an envelope addressed to Mr. Dooley, and containing a bit of pasteboard upon which was written, in the charming hand of Dolly:

> Mrs. R. Dolly-Rassendyll.
> At Home.
>   The Hippodorium.
> Tuesday Afternoon.

The response was gratifyingly immediate.

The next morning Dolly's mail contained Mr. Dooley's card, which read as follows:

144

"'I MUST SEE HIM,' SAID DOLLY"

DOLLY VISITS CHICAGO

```
Mr. Dooley.
At Work.
Every Day.          Archie Road.
```

"Which means?" said Dolly, tossing the card across the table to me.

"That if you want to see Dooley you'll have to call upon him at his place of business. It's a saloon, I believe," I observed. "Or a club—most American saloons are clubs, I understand."

"I wonder if there's a ladies' day there?" laughed Dolly. "If there isn't, perhaps I'd better not."

And I of course agreed, for when Dolly thinks perhaps she'd better not, I always agree with her, particularly when the thing is a trifle unconventional.

"I am sorry," she said, as we reached the conclusion. "To visit Chicago without meeting Mr. Dooley strikes me as like making the Mediterranean trip without seeing Gibraltar."

But we were not to be disappointed,
after all, for that afternoon who should
call but the famous philosopher himself,
accompanied by his friend Mr. Hennessey.
They were ushered into our little parlor,
and Dolly received them radiantly.

"Iv coorse," said Dooley, "I hatter
come t' see me new-found cousin. Hennessey here says, he says, 'She ain't yer
cousin,' he says; but whin I read yer
car-r-rd over th' second time, an' see yer
na-a-ame was R. Dooley-Rassendyll, wid th'
hifalution betwixt th' Dooley an' th' Rassendyll, I says, 'Hennessey,' I says, 'that
shmall bit iv a coupler in that na-a-ame
means only wan thing,' I says. 'Th' la-
ady,' I says, 'was born a Dooley, an' 's
prood iv it,' I says, 'as she'd ought to be,'
I says. 'Shure enough,' says Hennessey;
'but they's Dooleys an' Dooleys,' he says.
'Is she Roscommon or Idunnaw?' he says.
'I dinnaw meself,' I says, 'but whichiver
she is,' I says, 'I'm goin' to see her,' I
says. 'Anny wan that can feel at home
in a big hotel like the Hippojorium,' I
148

says, 'is wort' lookin' at, if only for the
curawsity of it,' I says. Are ye here for
long ?"

"We are just passing through," said
Dolly, with a pleased smile.

"It's a gud pla-ace for that," said Dooley. "Thim as pass troo Chicago gineral-
ly go awaa pleased, an' thim as stays t'ink
it's th' only pla-ace in th' worruld, gud
luk to 'em ! for, barrin' Roscommon an'
New York, it's th' only pla-ace I have
anny use for. Is yer hoosband anny relation t' th' dood in the *Prizner iv Cin-
ders ?*"

I laughed quietly, but did not resent
the implication. I left Dolly to her fate.

"He is the very same person," said
Dolly.

"I t'ought as much," said Dooley, eying
me closely. "Th' strorberry mark on his
hair sort of identified him," he added.
"Cousin Roopert, I ta-ak ye by the hand.
Ye was a bra-ave lad in th' first book, an'
a dom'd fool in th' second ; but I read th'
second first, and th' first lasht, so whin I
149

left ye ye was all right. I t'ought ye was dead ?"

"No," said I. "I am only dead in the sense that Mr. Hope has no further use for me."

"A wise mon, that Mr. Ant'ny Hawp," said Dooley. "Whin I write me book," he continued, "I'm goin' t' shtop short whin folks have had enough."

"Oh, indeed !" cried Dolly, enthusiastically. "Are you writing a book, Mr. Dooley ? I am so glad."

"Yis," said Dooley, deprecatingly, yet pleased by Dolly's enthusiasm. "I'm half finished already. That is to say, I've made th' illusthrations. An' the publishers have accepted the book on th' stringth iv them."

"Really ?" said Dolly. "Do you really draw ?"

"Nawm," said Dooley. "I niver drew a picture in me life."

"He draws corks," put in Hennessey. "He's got a pull that bates—"

"Hennessey," interrupted Mr. Dooley, "since whin have ye been me funnygraph ?

Whin me cousin ashks me riddles, I'll tell her th' answers. G' down-shtairs an' get a cloob san'wich an' ate yourself to death. Char-rge it to—er—char-rge it to Misther Rassendyll here — me cousin Roop, be marritch. He looks liks a soft t'ing."

Hennessey subsided and showed an inclination to depart, and I, not liking to see a well-meaning person thus sat upon, tried to be pleasant to him.

"Don't go just yet, Mr. Hennessey," said I. "I should like to talk to you."

"Mr. Rassendyll," he replied, "I'm not goin' just yet, but an invitation to join farces with cne iv the Hippojorium's cloob sandwhiches is too much for me. I must accept. Phwat is the noomber iv your shweet ?"

I gave him the number, and Hennessey departed. Before he went, however, he comforted me somewhat by saying that he too was "a puppit in th' han's iv an auter. Ye've got to do," said he, "whativer ye're sint t' do. I'm told ye've killed a million Germans—bless ye !—but ye're

151

nawthin' but a facthory hand afther all.
I'm th' background iv Dooley. If Dooley
wants to be smar-rt, I've got t' play th'
fool. It's the same with you; only you've
had yer chance at a printcess, later on
pla-acin' the la-ady in a 'nonymous p'sition
—which is enough for anny man, Dooley
or no Dooley."

Hennessey departed in search of his
club sandwich, which was subsequently
alluded to in my bill, and for which I paid
with pleasure, for Hennessey is a good fellow. I then found myself listening to the
conversation between Dolly and Dooley.

" Roscommon, of course," Dolly was saying. What marvellous adaptability that
woman has ! " How could you think, my
dear cousin, that I belonged to the farmer
Dooleys ?"

" I t'ought as much," said Mr. Dooley,
genially, "now that I've seen ye. Whin
you put th' wor-rds 'at home' on yer
car-rd, I had me doots. No Dooley iv th'
right sor-rt iver liked annyt'ing a landlord gave him ; an' whin y' expreshed satis-

faction wid th' Hippojorium, I didn't at
first t'ink ye was a true Dooley. Since I've
seen ye, I love ye properly, ma'am—like
th' cousin I am. I've read iv ye, just as
I've read iv yer hoosband, Cousin Roopert
here be marritch, in th' biojographies of
Mr. Ant'ny Hawp, an' while I cudn't help
likin' ye, I must say I didn't t'ink ye was
very deep on th' surface, an' when I read
iv your elopin' with Cousin Roop, I says
to Hennessey, I says, 'Hennessey,' I says,
'that's all right; they'd bote iv 'em better
die, but let us not be asashinators,' I says;
'let 'em be joined in marritch. That's
punishment enough,' I says to Hennessey.
Ye see, Miss Dooley, I have been marrit
meself."

" But I have found married life far from
punishment," I heard Dolly say. " I fear
you're a sad pessimist, Mr. Dooley," she
added.

" I'm not," Mr. Dooley replied. " I'm
a Jimmycrat out an' out, if ye refer to me
politics; but if your remark is a reflec-
tion on me religion, let me tell ye, ma'am,

that, like all me countrymen in this beautiful land, I'm a Uni-tarrian, an' prood iv it."

I ventured to interpose at this point.

"Dooley," said I, "your cousin Roop,
as you call him, is very glad to meet you,
whatever your politics or your religion."

"Mosht people are," said he, dryly.

"That shows good taste," said I. "But
how about your book? It has been accepted on the strength of its illustrations,
you say. How about them? Can we see
them anywhere? Are they on exhibition?"

"You can not only see thim, but you
can drink 'em free anny time you come
out to Archie Road," Dooley replied, cor-
dially."

"Drink—a picture?" I asked.

"Yis," said Dooley. "Didn't ye iver
hear iv dhrinkin' in a picture, Cousin Roopert? Didn't ye hear th' tark about th'
'Angelus' whin 'twas here? Ye cud hear
th' bells ringin' troo th' paint iv it. Ye
cud almost hear th' couple in front just
back iv th' varnish quar'lin as t'whether
'twas th' Angelus er the facthery bell that

"'KAPE YOUR HOOSBAND HOME'"

was goin' off. 'Twas big an' little felt th' inflooance iv Misther Miller's jaynius, just be lukin' at ut—though as fer me, th' fir-rst time I see the t'ing I says, says I, 'Is ut lukin' for bait to go fishin' with they are?' I says. 'Can't ye hear the pealin' iv the bells?' says Hennessey, who was with me. 'That an' more,' I says. 'I can hear the pealin' o' th' petayties,' I says. 'Do ye dhrink in th' feelin' iv it?' says Hennessey. 'Naw, t'ank ye,' I says. 'I'm not thirsty,' I says. 'Besides, I've swore off dhrinkin' ile-paintin's,' I says. 'Wather-coolers is guð enough fer me,' I says. An' wid that we wint back to the Road. But that was th' fir-rst time I iver heard iv dhrinkin' a work iv ar-rt.''

"But some of the things you—ah—you Americans crink," put in Dolly, "are works of art, my dear Mr. Dooley. Your cousin Rupert gave me a cocktail at dinner last night—"

"Ye've hit ut, Miss Dooley," returned the philosopher, with a beautiful enthusiasm. "Ye've hit ut square. I see

157

now y're a thrue Dooley. An' wid yer
kind permission I'll dedicate me book to
ye. Ut's cocktails that book's about,
ma'am. *Fifty Cocktails I Have Met* is th'
na-ame iv ut. An' whin I submitted th'
mannyscrip' wid th' illusthrations to the
publisher, he dhrank 'em all, an' he says,
'Dooley,' he says, 'ut's a go. I'll do yer
book,' he says, 'an' I'll pay ye wan hoondred an' siventy-five per cent.,' he says.
'Set 'em up again, Dooley,' he says ; an'
I mixed 'em. 'I t'ink, Dooley,' he says,
afther goin' troo th' illusthrations th' second toime—'I t'ink,' he says, 'ye'd ought
to get two hoondred an' wan per cent. on
th' retail price iv th' book,' he says.
'Can't I take a bottle iv these illusthrations to me office ?' he says. 'I'd like to
look 'em over,' he says ; an' I mixed 'im
up a quar-rt iv th' illusthrations to th'
chaphter on th' Mar-rtinney, an' sent him
back to his partner in th' ambylanch."

"I shall look forward to the publica-
tion of your book with much interest, Mr.
Dooley," said Dolly. "Now that I have

MIXING ILLUSTRATIONS

discovered our cousinship, I am even more interested in you than I was before; and let me tell you that, before I met you, I thought of you as the most vital figure in American humor that has been produced in many years."

"I know nothin' iv American humor," said Dooley, "for I haven't met anny lately, an' I know nothin' iv victuals save what I ate, an' me appytite is as satisfoid wid itself as Hobson is wid th' kisses brawt onto him by th' sinkin' iv th' Merrimickinley. But for you an' Misther Rassendyll, ma'am, I've nothin' but good wishes an' ah—illusthrations to me book whenever ye give yer orders. Kape your hoosband home, Miss Dooley," he added. "He's scrapped wanst too often already wi' th' Ruraltarriers, an' he's been killed off wanst by Mr. Ant'ny Hawp; but he'll niver die if ye only kape him home. If he goes out he'll git fightin' agin. If he attimpts a sayquil to the sayquil, he's dead sure enough!"

And with this Dolly and Dooley parted.

For myself, Rupert Rassendyll, I think Dooley's advice was good, and as long as Dolly will keep me home, I'll stay. For is it not better to be the happy husband of Dolly of the Dialogues, than to be going about like a knight of the Middle Ages clad in the evening dress of the nineteenth century, doing impossible things?

As for Dooley's impression of Dolly, I can only quote what I heard he had said after meeting her.

"She's a Dooley sure," said he, being novel to compliment. And I am glad she is, for despite the charms of Flavia of pleasant memory, there's nobody like Dolly for me, and if Dolly can only be acknowledged by the Dooleys, her fame, I am absolutely confident, is assured.

IX

IN WHICH YELLOW JOURNALISM CREEPS IN

THE applause which followed the reading of the Dooley Dialogue showed very
clearly that, among the diners at least,
neither Dooley nor Dolly had waned in
popularity. If the dilution, the faint echo
of the originals, evoked such applause, how
potent must have been the genius of the
men who first gave life to Dooley and the
fair Dolly !

"That's good stuff, Greenwich," said
Billie Jones. "You must have eaten a
particularly digestible meal. Now for the
tenth ball. Who has it ?"

"I," said Dick Snobbe, rising majesti-
cally from his chair. "And I can tell you
what it is ; I had a tough time of it in my

dream, as you will perceive when I recite
to you the story of my experiences at the
battle of Manila."

"Great Scott, Dick!" cried Bedford
Parke. "You weren't in that, were you?"

"Sir," returned Dick, "I was not only
in it, I was the thing itself. I was the
war correspondent of the Sunday *Whirnal*,
attached to Dewey's fleet."

Whereupon the talented Mr. Snobbe
proceeded to read the following cable despatch from the special correspondent of
the *Whirnal:*

MANILA FALLS

THE SPANISH FLEET DESTROYED

THE SPECIAL CORRESPONDENT OF THE
WHIRNAL

AIDED BY COMMODORE DEWEY AND HIS FLEET

CAPTURES THE PHILIPPINES

MANILA, *May* 1, 1898. — I have glori-
ous news. I have this day destroyed the
Spanish fleet and captured the Philippine
Islands. According to my instructions

164

from the City Editor of the *Whirnal*, I
boarded the *Olympia*, the flag-ship of the
fleet under Commodore Dewey at Hong-
kong, on Wednesday last. Upon reading
my credentials the Commodore immediately surrendered the command of the
fleet to me, and retired to his state-room,
where he has since remained. I deemed
it well to keep him there until after the
battle was over, fearing lest he should an-
noy me with suggestions, and not knowing but that he might at any time spread
dissension among the officers and men,
who, after the habit of seamen, frequently
manifest undue affection and sympathy
for a deposed commander. I likewise,
according to your wishes, concealed from
the officers and crew the fact that the
Commodore had been deposed, furthering
the concealment by myself making up as
Dewey. Indeed, it was not until after
the battle this morning that any but
Dewey and the ship's barber were aware
of the substitution, since my disguise was
perfect. The ship's barber I had to take

into my confidence, for unfortunately on
leaving Hong-kong I had forgotten to
provide myself with a false mustache, so
that in concealing the deposition of the
Commodore by myself assuming his per-
sonality I was compelled to have the gentleman's mustache removed from his upper lip and transferred to my own. This
the barber did with neatness and despatch,
I having first chloroformed the Commodore, from whom some resistance might
have been expected, owing to his peculiar
temperament. Fortunately the fellow was
an expert wig-maker, and within an hour
of the shaving of Dewey I was provided
with a mustache which could not fail to
be recognized as the Commodore's, since it
was indeed that very same object. When
five hundred miles at sea I dropped the
barber overboard, fearing lest he should
disturb my plans by talking too much. I
hated to do it, but in the interest of the
Whirnal I hold life itself as of little con-
sequence, particularly if it is the life of
some one else — and who knows but the

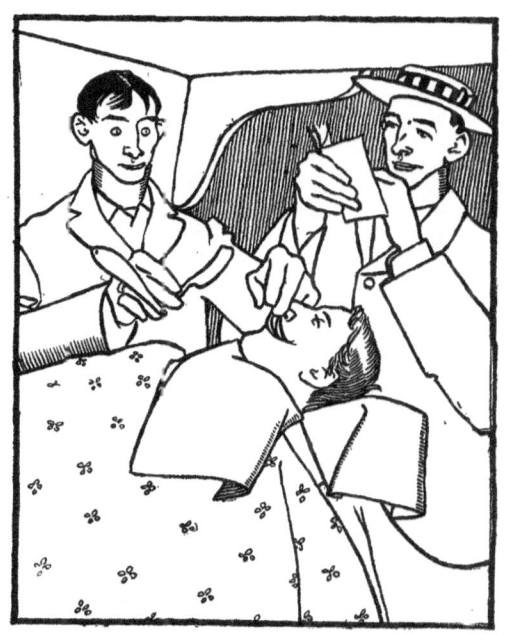

THE SHIP'S BARBER AT WORK

poor fellow was an expert swimmer, and has by this time reached Borneo or some other bit of dry land ? He was alive when I last saw him, and yelling right lustily. If it so happen that he has swum ashore some-where, kindly let me know at your con-venience ; for beneath a correspondent's exterior I have a warm heart, and it some-times troubles me to think that the poor fellow may have foundered, since the sea was stressful and the nearest dry point was four hundred and sixty knots away to S.E. by N.G., while the wind was blow-ing N.W. by N.Y.C. & H.R.R. But to my despatch.

Dewey done for, despoiled of his mus-tache and rifled of his place, with a heavy sea running and a dense fog listing to starboard, I summoned my officers to the flag-ship, and, on the evening of April 30th, the fog-horns of Cavité having indicated the approach of the Philippine coast, gave them, one and all, their final instructions. These were, in brief, never to do anything without consulting with me.

THE DREAMERS: A CLUB

"'To facilitate matters, gentlemen," said I, ordering an extra supply of grog for the captains, and milk punches for the lieutenants, " we must connect the various vessels of the fleet with telephone wires. Who will undertake this perilous duty?"

They rose up as one man, and, with the precision of a grand-opera chorus, replied: "Commodore"—for they had not penetrated my disguise—"call upon us. If you will provide the wires and the 'phones, we will do the rest." And they followed these patriotic words with cheers for me.

Their heroism so affected me that I had difficulty in frowning upon the head-butler's suggestion that my glass should be filled again.

"Gentlemen," said I, huskily—for I was visibly affected—"I have provided for all. I could not do otherwise and remain myself. You will find ten thousand miles of wire and sixty-six telephones in the larder."

That night every ship in the fleet was provided with telephone service. I appointed the *Olympia* to be the central office, so that I might myself control all the messages, or at least hear them as they passed to and fro. In the absence of ladies from the fleet, I appointed a somewhat effeminate subaltern to the post of "Hello Officer," with complete control over the switch-board. And, as it transpired, this was a very wise precaution, because the central office was placed in the hold, and the poor little chap's courage was so inclined to ooze that in the midst of the fight he was content to sit below the water-line at his post, and not run about the promenade-deck giving orders while under fire. I have cabled the President about him, and have advised his promotion. His heroic devotion to the switch-board ought to make him a naval attaché to some foreign court, at least. I trust his bravery will ultimately result in his being sent to the Paris Exposition as charge d'affaires in the Erie Canal department of the New York State exhibit.

But to return to my despatch—which

from this point must disregard space and move quickly. Passing Cape Bolinao, we soon reached Subig Bay, fifty miles from Manila. Recognizing the cape by the crop of hemp on its brow, I rang up the *Boston* and the *Concord*.

"Search Subig Bay," I ordered.

"Who's this?" came the answer from the other end.

"Never mind who I am," said I. "Search Subig Bay for Spaniards."

"Hello!" said the *Boston*.

"Who the deuce are you?" cried the *Concord*.

"I'm seventeen-five-six," I replied, with some sarcasm, for that was not my number.

"I want sixteen-two-one," retorted the *Boston*.

"Ring off," said the *Concord*. "What do you mean by giving me seventeen-five-six?"

"Hello, *Boston* and *Concord*," I put in in commanding tones. "I'm Dewey."

This is the only false statement I ever

172

made, but it was in the interests of my country, and my reply was electrical in its effect. The *Boston* immediately blew off steam, and the *Concord* sounded all hands to quarters.

"What do you want, Commodore?" they asked simultaneously.

"Search Subig Bay for Spaniards, as I have already ordered you," I replied, "and woe be unto you if you don't find any."

"What do you want 'em for, Commodore?" asked the *Boston*.

"To engage, you idiot," I replied, scornfully. "What did you suppose—to teach me Spanish?"

Both vessels immediately piped all hands on deck and set off. Two hours later they returned, and the telephone subaltern reported, "No Spaniards found."

"Why not?" I demanded.

"All gone to Cuba," replied the *Boston*. "Shall we pipe all hands to Cuba?"

"Wires too short to penetrate without a bust," replied the *Concord*.

"On to Manila!" was my answer. "Ding

the torpedoes—go ahead! Give us Spaniards or give us death!"

These words inspired every ship in the line, and we immediately strained forward, except the *McCulloch*, which I despatched at once to Hong-kong to cable my last words to you in time for the Adirondack edition of your Sunday issue leaving New York Thursday afternoon.

The rest of us immediately proceeded. In a short while, taking advantage of the darkness for which I had provided by turning the clock back so that the sun by rising at the usual hour should not disclose our presence, we turned Corregidor and headed up the Boca Grande towards Manila. As we were turning Corregidor the telephone-bell rang, and somebody who refused to give his name, but stating that he was aboard the *Petrel*, called me up.

"Hello!" said I.

"Is this Dewey?" said the *Petrel*.

"Yes," said I.

"There are torpedoes ahead," said the *Petrel*.

174

"What of it ?" said I.

"How shall we treat 'em ?"

"Blow 'em off—to soda water," I answered, sarcastically.

"Thank you, sir," the *Petrel* replied, as she rang off.

Then somebody from the *Baltimore* rang me up.

"Commodore Dewey," said the *Baltimore,* "there are mines in the harbor."

"Well, what of it ?" I replied.

"What shall we do ?" asked the *Baltimore.*

"Treat them coldly, as they do in the Klondike," said I.

"But they aren't gold-mines," replied the *Baltimore.*

"Then salt 'em," said I, dryly. "Apply for a certificate of incorporation, water your stock, sell out, and retire."

"Thank you, Commodore," the *Baltimore* answered. "How many shares shall we put you down for ?"

"None," said I. "But if you'll use your surplus to start a life-insurance company, I'll take out a policy for forty-eight hours, and send you my demand note to pay for the first premium."

I mention this merely to indicate to your readers that I felt myself in a position of extreme peril, and did not forget my obligations to my family. It is a small matter, but if you will search the pages of history you will see that in the midst of the greatest dangers the greatest heroes have thought of apparently insignificant details.

At this precise moment we came in sight of the fortresses of Manila. Signalling the *Raleigh* to heave to, I left the flag-ship and jumped aboard the cruiser, where I discharged with my own hand the after-forecastle four-inch gun. The shot struck Corregidor, and, glancing off, as I had designed, caromed on the smoke-stack of the *Reina Cristina*, the flag-ship of Admiral Montojo. The Admiral, unaccustomed to such treatment, immediately got out of bed, and, putting on his pajamas, appeared on the bridge.

A CLEVER CAROM

"Who smoked our struck-stack?" he demanded, in broken English.

"The enemy," cried his crew, with some nervousness. I was listening to their words through the megaphone.

"Then let her sink," said he, clutching his brow sadly with his clinched fist. "Far be it from me to stay afloat in Manila Bay on the 1st of May, and so cast discredit on history!"

The *Reina Cristina* immediately sank, according to the orders of the Admiral, and I turned my attention to the *Don Juan de Austria*. Rowing across the raging channel to the *Baltimore*, I boarded her and pulled the lanyard of the port boom forty-two. The discharge was terrific.

"What has happened?" I asked, coolly, as the explosion exploded. "Did we hit her?"

"We did, your honor," said the Bo's'n's mate, "square in the eye; only, Commodore, it ain't a her this time—it's a him. It's the *Don Juan de*—"

179

"Never mind the sex," I cried. "Has she sank?"

"No, sir," replied the Bo's'n's mate, "she 'ain't sank yet. "She's a-waiting orders."

"Fly signals to sink," said I, sternly, for I had resolved that she should go down.

They did so, and the *Don Juan de Austria* immediately disappeared beneath the waves. Her commander evidently realized that I meant what I signalled.

"Are there any more of the enemy afloat?" I demanded, jumping from the deck of the *Baltimore* to that of the *Concord*.

"No, Commodore," replied the captain of the latter.

"Then signal the enemy to charter two more gunboats and have 'em sent out. I can't be put off with two boats when I'm ready to sink four," I replied.

The *Concord* immediately telephoned to the Spanish commandant at the Manila Café de la Paix, who as quickly chartered

SINKING THE *CASTILLA*

the *Castilla* and the *Velasco* — two very good boats that had recently come in in ballast with the idea of loading up with bananas and tobacco.

While waiting for these vessels to come out and be sunk, I ordered all hands to breakfast, thus reviving their falling courage. It was a very good breakfast, too. We had mush and hominy and potatoes in every style, beefsteak, chops, liver and bacon, chicken hash, buckwheat cakes and fish - balls, coffee, tea, rolls, toast, and brown bread.

Just as we were eating the latter the *Castilla* and *Velasco* came out. I fired my revolver at the *Castilla* and threw a fish-ball at the *Velasco*. Both immediately burst into flames.

Manila was conquered.

The fleet gone, the city fell. It not only fell, but slid, and by nightfall Old Glory waved over the citadel.

The foe was licked.

To-morrow I am to see Dewey again.

I think I shall resign to-night.

P.S.—Please send word to the magazines that all articles by Dewey must be written by Me. Terms, $500 per word. The strain has been worth it.

X

THE MYSTERY OF PINKHAM'S DIAMOND
STUD

Being the tale told by the holder of the eleventh ball,
Mr. Fulton Streete

"IT is the little things that tell in detective work, my dear Watson," said Sherlock Holmes as we sat over our walnuts
and coffee one bitter winter night shortly
before his unfortunate departure to Swit-
zerland, whence he never returned.

"I suppose that is so," said I, pulling
away upon the very excellent stogie which
mine host had provided — one made in
Pittsburg in 1885, and purchased by
Holmes, whose fine taste in tobacco had
induced him to lay a thousand of these
down in his cigar-cellar for three years,

and then keep them in a refrigerator, overlaid with a cloth soaked in Château Yquem wine for ten. The result may be better imagined than described. Suffice it to say that my head did not recover for three days, and the ash had to be cut off the stogie with a knife. "I suppose so, my dear Holmes," I repeated, taking my knife and cutting three inches of the stogie off and casting it aside, furtively, lest he should think I did not appreciate the excellence of the tobacco, "but it is not given to all of us to see the little things. Is it, now?"

"Yes," he said, rising and picking up the rejected portion of the stogie. "We all see everything that goes on, but we don't all know it. We all hear everything that goes on, but we are not conscious of the fact. For instance, at this present moment there is somewhere in this world a man being set upon by assassins and yelling lustily for help. Now his yells create a certain atmospheric disturbance. Sound is merely vibration, and, once set going, these vibrations will run on and on and on in ripples into the infinite—that is, they will never stop, and sooner or later these vibrations must reach our ears. We may not know it when they do, but they will do so none the less. If the man is in the next room, we will hear the yells almost simultaneously—not quite, but almost—with their utterance. If the man is in Timbuctoo, the vibrations may not reach us for a little time, according to the speed with which they travel. So with sight. Sight seems limited, but in reality it is not. *Vox populi, vox Dei.* If *vox,* why not *oculus?* It is a simple proposition, then, that the eye of the people being the eye of God, the eye of God being all-seeing, therefore the eye of the people is all-seeing—Q. E. D."

I gasped, and Holmes, cracking a walnut, gazed into the fire for a moment.

"It all comes down, then," I said, "to the question, who are the people?"

Holmes smiled grimly. "All men," he replied, shortly; "and when I say all men, I mean all creatures who can reason."

"Does that include women?" I asked.

"Certainly," he said. "Indubitably. The fact that women *don't* reason does not prove that they can't. I *can* go up in a balloon if I wish to, but I *don't*. I *can* read an American newspaper comic supplement, but I *don't*. So it is with women. Women can reason, and therefore they have a right to be included in the classification whether they do or don't."

"Quite so," was all I could think of to say at the moment. The extraordinary logic of the man staggered me, and I again began to believe that the famous mathematician who said that if Sherlock Holmes attempted to prove that five apples plus three peaches made four pears, he would not venture to dispute his conclusions, was wise. (This was the famous Professor Zoggenhoffer, of the Leipsic School of Moral Philosophy and Stenography.—ED.)

"Now you agree, my dear Watson," he

188

said, "that I have proved that we see everything?"

"Well—" I began.

"Whether we are conscious of it or not?" he added, lighting the gas-log, for the cold was becoming intense.

"From that point of view, I suppose so —yes," I replied, desperately.

"Well, then, this being granted, consciousness is all that is needed to make us fully informed on any point."

"No," I said, with some positiveness. "The American people are very conscious, but I can't say that generally they are well-informed."

I had an idea this would knock him out, as the Bostonians say, but counted without my host. He merely laughed.

"The American is only self-conscious. Therefore he is well-informed only as to self," he said.

"You've proved your point, Sherlock," I said. "Go on. What else have you proved?"

"That it is the little things that tell,"

189

he replied. "Which all men would realize
in a moment if they could see the little
things — and when I say ' if they could
see,' I of course mean if they could be
conscious of them."

"Very true," said I.

"And I have the gift of consciousness,"
he added.

I thought he had, and I said so. "But,"
I added, "give me a concrete example."
It had been some weeks since I had listened
to any of his detective stories, and I was
athirst for another.

He rose up and walked over to his
pigeon-holes, each labelled with a letter,
in alphabetical sequence.

"I have only to refer to any of these
to do so," he said. "Choose your letter."

"Really, Holmes," said I, "I don't
need to do that. I'll believe all you say.
In fact, I'll write it up and *sign my
name* to any statement you choose to
make."

"Choose your letter, Watson," he retorted. "You and I are on terms that

THE LAMP-POSTS WERE TWISTED

make flattery impossible. Is it F, J, P, Q, or Z ?"

He fixed his eye penetratingly upon me. It seemed for the moment as if I were hypnotized, and as his gaze fairly stabbed me with its intensity, through my mind there ran the suggestion " Choose J, choose J, choose J." To choose J became an obsession. To relieve my mind, I turned my eye from his and looked at the fire. Each flame took on the form of the letter J. I left my chair and walked to the window and looked out. The lamp-posts were twisted into the shape of the letter J. I returned, sat down, gulped down my brandy-and-soda, and looked up at the portraits of Holmes's ancestors on the wall. They were all J's. But I was resolved never to yield, and I gasped out, desperately,

"Z !"

"Thanks," he said, calmly. "Z be it. I thought you would. Reflex hypnotism, my dear Watson, is my forte. If I wish a man to choose Q, B takes hold upon him.

If I wish him to choose **K**, **A** fills his mind. Have you ever observed how the mind of man repels a suggestion and flees to something else, merely that it may demonstrate its independence of another mind ? Now I have been suggesting **J** to you, and you have chosen **Z**—"

"You misunderstood me," I cried, desperately. "I did not say **Z**; I said **P**."

"Quite so," said he, with an inward chuckle. "**P** was the letter I wished you to choose. If you had insisted upon **Z**, I should really have been embarrassed. See !" he added. He removed the green-ended box that rested in the pigeon-hole marked **Z**, and, opening it, disclosed an emptiness.

"I've never had a **Z** case. But **P**," he observed, quietly, "is another thing altogether."

Here he took out the box marked **P** from the pigeon-hole, and, opening it, removed the contents—a single paper which was carefully endorsed, in his own handwriting, "The Mystery of Pinkham's Diamond Stud."

"You could not have selected a better case, Watson," he said, as he unfolded the paper and scanned it closely. "One would almost think you had some prevision of the fact."

"I am not aware," said I, "that you ever told the story of Pinkham's diamond stud. Who was Pinkham, and what kind of a diamond stud was it—first-water or Rhine?"

"Pinkham," Holmes rejoined, "was an American millionaire, living during business hours at Allegheny City, Pennsylvania, where he had to wear a brilliant stud to light him on his way through the streets, which are so dark and sooty that an ordinary search-light would not suffice. In his leisure hours, however, he lived at the Hotel Walledup-Hysteria, in New York, where he likewise had to wear the same diamond stud to keep him from being a marked man. Have you ever visited New York, Watson?"

THE DREAMERS: A CLUB

" No," said I.

" Well, when you do, spend a little of
your time at the Walledup-Hysteria. It
is a hotel with a population larger than
that of most cities, with streets running
to and from all points of the compass ;
where men and women eat under conditions that Lucullus knew nothing of ;
where there is a carpeted boulevard on
which walk all sorts and conditions of
men ; where one pays one's bill to the
dulcet strains of a string orchestra that
woo him into a blissful forgetfulness of
its size ; and where, by pressing a button
in the wall, you may summon a grand
opera, or a porter who on request will
lend you enough money to enable you and
your family to live the balance of your
days in comfort. In America men have
been known to toil for years to amass a
fortune for the one cherished object of
spending a week in this Olympian spot,
and then to be content to return to their
toil and begin life anew, rich only in the
memory of its luxuries. It was here that

I spent my time when, some years ago, I went to the United States to solve the now famous Piano Case. You will remember how sneak thieves stole a grand piano from the residence of one of New York's first families, while the family was dining in the adjoining room. While in the city, and indeed at the very hotel in which I stopped, and which I have described, Pinkham's diamond stud disappeared, and, hearing that I was a guest at the Walledup-Hysteria, the owner appealed to me to recover it for him. I immediately took the case in hand. Drastic questioning of Pinkham showed that beyond all question he had lost the stud in his own apartment. He had gone down to dinner, leaving it on the centre-table, following the usual course of most millionaires, to whom diamonds are of no particular importance. Pinkham wanted this one only because of its associations. Its value, $80,000, was a mere bagatelle in his eyes.

" Now of course, if he positively left it on the table, it must have been taken by some one who had entered the room. Investigation proved that the maid, a valet, a fellow-millionaire from Chicago, and Pinkham's children had been the only ones to do this. The maid and the valet were above suspicion. Their fees from guests were large enough to place them beyond the reach of temptation. I questioned them closely, and they convinced me at once of their innocence by conducting me through the apartments of other guests wherein tiaras of diamonds and necklaces of pearls — ropes in very truth — rubies, turquoise, and emerald ornaments of price-less value, were scattered about in reck-less profusion.

"'D' yez t'ink oi'd waste me toime on an eighty-t'ousand-dollar shtood, wid all dhis in soight and moine for the thrubble uv swipin' ut ?' said the French maid.

"I acquitted her at once, and the valet similarly proved his innocence, only with less of an accent, for he was supposed to be English, and not French, as was the maid, although they both came from Dub-

HOLMES IN DISGUISE INTERVIEWS WATTLES

lin. This narrowed the suspects down to Mr. Jedediah Wattles, of Chicago, and the children. Naturally I turned my attention to Wattles. A six-year-old boy and a four-year-old girl could hardly be suspected of stealing a diamond stud. So drawing on Pinkham for five thousand dollars to pay expenses, I hired a room in a tenement-house in Rivington Street—a squalid place it was — disguised myself with an oily, black, burglarious mustache, and dressed like a comic-paper gambler. Then I wrote a note to Wattles, asking him to call, saying that I could tell him something to his advantage. He came, and I greeted him like a pal. 'Wattles,' said I, 'you've been working this game for a long time, and I know all about you. You are an ornament to the profession, but we diamond-thieves have got to combine. Understand?' 'No, I don't,' said he. 'Well, I'll tell you,' said I. 'You're a man of good appearance, and I ain't, but I know where the diamonds are. If we work together, there's millions in it.

I'll spot the diamonds, and you lift 'em, eh? You can do it,' I added, as he began to get mad. 'The ease with which you got away with old Pinky's stud, that I've been trying to pull for myself for years, shows me that.'

"I was not allowed to go further. Wattles's indignation was great enough to prove that it was not he who had done the deed, and after he had thrashed me out of my disguise, I pulled myself together and said, 'Mr. Wattles, I am convinced that you are innocent.' As soon as he recognized me and realized my object in sending for him, he forgave me, and, I must say, treated me with great consideration.

"But my last clew was gone. The maid, the valet, and Wattles were proved innocent. The children alone remained, but I could not suspect them. Nevertheless, on my way back to the hotel I bought some rock-candy, and, after reporting to Pinkham, I asked casually after the children.

"'YOU DID TOO!' SAID POLLY".

"'They're pretty well,' said Pinkham. 'Billie's complaining a little, and the doctor fears appendicitis, but Polly's all right. I guess Billie's all right too. The seventeen-course dinners they serve in the children's dining-room here aren't calculated to agree with Billie's digestion, I reckon.'

"'I'd like to see 'em,' said I. 'I'm very fond of children.'

"Pinkham immediately called the youngsters in from the nursery. 'Guess what I've got,' I said, opening the package of rock-candy. 'Gee!' cried Billie, as it caught his eye. 'Gimme some!' 'Who gets first piece?' said I. 'Me!' cried both. 'Anybody ever had any before?' I asked. 'He has,' said Polly, pointing to Billie. The boy immediately flushed up. ''Ain't, neither!' he retorted. 'Yes you did, too,' said Polly. '*You swallered that piece pop left on the centre-table the other night!*' 'Well, anyhow, it was only a little piece,' said Billie. 'An' it tasted like glass,' he added. Handing the candy to Polly, I picked Billie up and carried him to his father.

" 'Mr. Pinkham,' said I, handing the boy over, ' here is your diamond. It has not been stolen; it has merely been swallowed.' 'What?' he cried. And I explained. The stud mystery was explained. Mr. Pinkham's boy had eaten it."

Holmes paused.

" Well, I don't see how that proves your point," said I. " You said that it was the little things that told—"

"So it was," said Holmes. "If Polly hadn't told—"

"Enough," I cried; "it's on me, old man. We will go down to Willis's and have some Russian caviare and a bottle of Burgundy."

Holmes put on his hat and we went out together. It is to get the money to pay Willis's bill that I have written this story of "The Mystery of Pinkham's Diamond Stud."

XI

LANG TAMMAS AND DRUMSHEUGH SWEAR OFF

A tale of dialect told by Mr. Berkeley Hights, holder of the twelfth ball

" Hoot mon !"

The words rang out derisively on the cold frosty air of Drumtochty, as Lang Tammas walked slowly along the street, looking for the residence of Drumsheugh. The effect was electrical. Tammas stopped short, and turning about, scanned the street eagerly to see who it was that had spoken. But the highway was deserted, and the old man shook his stick, as if at an imaginary foe.

"I'll hoot-mon the dour eediot that's eensoolted a veesitor to Drumtochty !" he shouted. "I haena brought me faithfu' stock for naething!" he added.

He glared about, now at this closed window, now at that, as if inviting his enemy to come forth and be punished, but seeing no signs of life, turned again to resume his walk, muttering angrily to himself. It was indeed hardly to be tolerated that he, one of the great characters of fiction, should be thus jeered at, as he thought, while on a friendly pilgrimage from Thrums to Drumtochty, the two rival towns in the affections of the consumers of modern letters; and having walked all the way from his home at Thrums, Lang Tammas was tired, and therefore in no mood to accept even a mild affront, much less an insult.

He had scarcely covered ten paces, however, when the same voice, with a harsh cackling laugh, again broke the stillness of the street:

"Gang awa', gang awa'—ha, ha, ha!"

Tammas rushed into the middle of the way and picked up a stone.

" ' HOOT MON ! ' "

"Pit your bogie pate oot o' your weendow, me gillie!" he cried. "I'll gie it a garry crack. Pit it oot, I say! Pit it oot."

And the old man drew himself back into an attitude which would have defied the powers of Phidias to reproduce in marble, the stone poised accurately and all too ready to be hurled.

"Ye ramshackle macloonatic!" he cried. "Standin' in a weendow, where nane may see, an' heepin' eensoolts on deecint fowk. Pit it oot—pit it oot—an' get it crackit!"

The reply was instant:

"Gang awa', gang awa'—ha, ha, ha!"

Had Lang Tammas been a creation of Lever, he would at this point have removed his coat and his hat and thrown them down violently to earth, and then have whacked the walk three times with the stout stick he carried in his right hand, as a preliminary to the challenge which followed. But Tammas was not Irish, and therefore not impulsive. He was Scotch—as Scotch as ever was. Wherefore he re-

moved his hat, and, after dusting it carefully, hung it up on a convenient hook;
took off his coat and folded it neatly;
picked up his "faithfu' steck," and observed:

"I hae naething to do that's of eempor-
tance. Drumsheugh can wait, an' sae can
ee. Pit it oot, pit it oot! Here I am,
an' here I stay until ye pit it oot to be
crackit."

"Gang awa', gang awa'—ha, ha, ha!"
came the reply.

Lang Tammas turned on the instant to
the sources of the sound. He fixed his
eyes sternly on the very window whence
he thought the words had issued.

"Number twenty-three, saxth floor,"
he muttered to himself. "I will call, and
then we shall see what we *shall* see; and
if what we see gets off wi'oot a thorough
'hootin',' then I dinna ken me beezniss."

Hastily discarding his outward wrath,
and assuming such portions of his garments as went with his society manner,
Tammas walked into the lobby of the

"A SWEET-FACED NURSE APPEARED"

apartment-house in which his assumed insulter lived. He pushed the electric button in, and shortly a sweet-faced nurse appeared.

"Who are you?" she asked.

"Me," said Lang Tammas, somewhat abashed. "I've called too see the head o' the hoose."

"I am sorry," said the trained nurse, bursting into tears, "but the head of the house is at the point of death, sir, and cannot see you until to-morrow. Call around about ten o'clock."

"Hoots an' toots!" sighed Lang Tammas. "Canna we Scuts have e'er a story wi'oot somebody leein' at the point o' death! It's most affectin', but doonricht wearin' on the constitootion."

"Was there anything you wished to say to him?" asked the nurse.

"Oh, aye!" returned Lang Tammas. "I dinna ken hoo to deny that I hed that to say to him, an' to do to him as weel. I'm a vairy truthfu' mon, young lady, an' if ye must be told, I've called to wring his

garry neck for dereesively gee'in an un-
offending veesitor frae Thrums by yelling
deealect at him frae the hoose-tops."

"Are you sure it was here?" asked the
nurse, anxiously, the old gentleman seemed
so deeply in earnest.

"Sure? Oh, aye—pairfectly," replied
Lang Tammas; but even as he spoke, the
falsity of his impression was proved by the
same strident voice that had so offended
before, coming from the other side of the
street :

"What a crittur ye are, ye cow! What
a crittur ye are!"

"Soonds are hard to place, ma'am," said
Lang Tammas, jerking about as if he had
been shot. It was a very hard position for
the old man, for, with the immediate need
for an apology to the nurse, there rushed
over him an overwhelming wave of anger.
Hitherto it was merely a suspicion that he
was being made sport of that had irritated
him, but this last outburst—"What a crittur ye are, ye cow!"—was convincing evidence that it was to him that the insults

were addressed; for in Thrums it is history that Hendry and T'nowhead and Jim McTaggart frequently greeted Lang Tammas's jokes with "Oh, ye cow!" and "What a crittur ye are!" But the old man was equal to the emergency, and fixing one eye upon the house opposite and the other upon the sweet-faced nurse, he darted glances that should kill at his persecutor, and at the same time apologized for disturbing the nurse. The latter he did gracefully.

"Ye look aweary, ma'am," he said. "An' if the head o' the hoose maun dee, may he dee immejiately, that ye may rest soon."

And with this, pulling his hat down over his forehead viciously, he turned and sped swiftly across the way. The nurse gazed anxiously after him, and in her secret soul wondered if she would not better send for Jamie McQueen, the town constable. Poor Tammas's eye was really so glaring, and his whole manner so manifestly that of a man exasperated to the

verge of madness, that she considered
him somewhat in the light of a menace
to the public safety. She was not at all
reassured, either, when Tammas, having
reached the other side of the street, began
gesticulating wildly, shaking his "faithfu' steck " at the façade of the confront-
ing flat-house. But an immediate realization of the condition of the sick man
above led her to forego the attempt to
protect the public safety, and closing the
door softly to, she climbed the weary
stairs to the sixth floor, and soon forgot
the disturbing trial of the morning in
reading to her patient certain inspiring
chapters from the Badminton edition of
Haggert's Chase of Heretics, relieved with
the lighter *Rules of Golf ; or, Auld Putt
Idylls*, by the Rev. Ian McCrockett, one
of the most exquisitely confusing humor-
ous works ever published in the High-
lands.

Lang Tammas meanwhile was addressing an invisible somebody in the building
over the way, and in no uncertain tones.

"If I were not a geentlemon and a humorist," he said, impressively, agitating his stick nervously at the building front, "I could say much that nae Scut may say. But were I nae Scut, I'd say this to ye: 'Ye have all the eelements of a confairmed heeritic. Ye've nae sense of deecint fun. Ye're not a man for a' that, as most men air—ye're an ass, plain and simple, wi' naether the plainness nor the simpleecity o' the individual that Balaam rode. Further—more—'"

What Lang Tammas would have said furthermore had he not been a Scot the world will never know, for from the other side of the street—farther along, however—came the squawking voice again:

"Gang awa', gang awa', ye crittur, ye cow! Hoot mon—hoot mon—hoot mon! Gang awa', gang awa'!" And this was followed by a raucous cry, which might or might not have been Scottish, but which was, in any event, distinctly maddening. And even as the previous insults had electrified poor Tammas, so this last petrified him, and he stood for an appreciable length of time absolutely transfixed. His mind was a curious study. His coming had been prompted entirely by the genial spirit which throbbed beneath his stony Scottish exterior. For a long time he had been a resident of the most conspicuous Scotch town in all literature, and he was himself its accepted humorist. Then on a sudden Thrums had a rival. Drumtochty sprang forth, and in the matter of pathos, if not humor, ran Thrums hard ; and Lang Tammas, attracted to Drumsheugh, had come this distance merely to pay his respects, and to see what manner of man the real Drumsheugh was.

And this was his reception ! To be laughed at—he, a Scotch humorist ! Had any one ever laughed at a Scotch humorist before ? Never. Was not the test of humor in Scotland the failure to laugh of the hearer of the jest ? Would Scotch humor ever prove great if not taken seriously ? Oh, aye ! Hendry never laughed

TAMMAS MEETS DRUMSHAUGH

at his jokes, and Hendry knew a joke when he saw one. McTaggart never smiled at Lang Tammas; and as for the little Minister—he knew what was due to the humorist of Thrums, as well as to himself, and enjoyed the exquisite humor of Tammas with a reserve well qualified to please the Presbytery and the Congregation.

How long Lang Tammas would have stood petrified no man may say; but just then who should come along but the person he had come to call upon — Drumsheugh himself.

"*Knox et prœterea nihil!*" he exclaimed. "What in Glasgie hae we here ?"

Lang Tammas turned upon him.

"Ye hae nowt in Glasgie here," he said, sternly. "Ye hae a vairy muckle pit-oot veesitor, wha hae coom on an airand o' good-will to be gret wi' eensoolts."

"Eensoolts ?" retorted Drumsheugh. "Eensoolts, ye say ? An' wha hae bin eensooltin' ye ?"

"That I know nowt of, save that he be

a doonricht foo' a - heepin' his deealect upon me head," said Lang Tammas.

"And wha are ye to be so seensitive o' deealect?" demanded Drumsheugh.

"My name is Lang Tammas—"

"O' Thrums?" cried Drumsheugh.

"Nane ither," said Tammas.

Drumsheugh burst into an uproarious fit of laughter.

"The humorist?" he cried, catching his sides.

"Nane ither," said Tammas, gravely. "And wha are ye?"

"Me? Oh, I'm—Drumsheugh o' Drumtochty," he replied. "Come along hame wi' me. I'll gie ye that to make the eensoolt seem a compliment."

And the two old men walked off together.

An hour later, on their way to the kirk, Drumsheugh observed that after the service was over he would go with Lang Tammas and seek out the man who had insulted him and "gie" him a drubbing, which invitation Tammas was nothing loath to accept. Reverently the two new-made friends walked into the kirk and sat themselves down on the side aisle. A hymn was sung, and the minister was about to read from the book, when the silence of the church was broken by a shrill voice :

"Hoot mon! Hoot mon!"

Tammas clutched his stick. The voice was the same, and here it had penetrated the sacred precincts of the church! Nowhere was he safe from insult. Drumsheugh looked up, startled, and the voice began again :

"Gang awa' a-that, a-that, a-that — gang awa'! Oh, ye crittur! oh, ye cow!"

And then a titter ran through that solemn crowd; for, despite the gravity of the situation, even John Knox himself must have smiled. A great green parrot had flown in at one of the windows, and had perched himself on the pulpit, where, with front undismayed, he addressed the minister :

"Gang awa', gang awa'!" he cried, and

P 225

preened himself. "Hoot mon, gang awa'!"

"*Knox nobiscum!*" ejaculated Drumsheugh. "It's Moggie McPiggert's pairrut," and he chuckled; and then, as Lang Tammas realized the situation, even he smiled broadly. He had been insulted by a parrot only, and the knowledge of it made him feel better.

The bird was removed and the service proceeded; and later, when it was over, as the two old fellows walked back to Drumsheugh's house in the gathering shades of the night, Lang Tammas said:

"I acquet Drumtochty o' its eensoolts, Drumsheugh, but I've lairnt a lesson this day."

"What's that?" asked Drumsheugh.

"When pairruts speak Scutch deealect, it's time we Scuts gae it oop," said Tammas.

"I think so mysel'," agreed Drumsheugh. "But hoo express our thochts?"

"I dinna ken for ye," said Lang Tammas, "but for me, mee speakee heathen Chinee this timee on."

"Vairy weel," returned Drumsheugh. "Vairy weel; I dinna ken heathen Chinee, but I hae some acqueentance wi' the tongue o' sairtain Amairicans, and that I'll speak from this day on—it's vairy weel called the Bowery eediom, and is a judeecious mixture o' English, Irish, and Volapeck."

And from that time on Lang Tammas and Drumsheugh spoke never another word of Scotch dialect; and while Tammas never quite mastered pidgin-English, or Drumsheugh the tongue of Fadden, they lived happily ever after, which in a way proves that, after all, the parrot is a useful as well as an ornamental bird.

XII

CONCLUSION—LIKEWISE MR. BILLY JONES

THE cheers which followed the narration of the curious resolve of Lang Tammas and Drumsheugh were vociferous, and Berkeley Hights sat down with a flush of pleasure on his face. He construed these as directed towards himself and his contribution to the diversion of the evening. It never entered into his mind that the applause involved a bit of subtle appreciation of the kindness of Tammas and of Drumsheugh to the reading public in thus declining to give them more of something of which they had already had enough.

When the cheers had subsided Mr.

CONCLUSION

Jones rose from his chair and congratulated the club upon its exhibit.

"Even if you have but faintly re-echoed the weaknesses of the strong," he said, "you have done well, and I congratulate you. It is not every man in your walk in life who can write as grammatically as you have dreamed. I have failed to detect in any one of the stories or poems thus far read a single grammatical error, and I have no doubt that the manuscripts that you have read from are gratifyingly free from mistakes in spelling as well, so that, from a newspaper man's stand-point, I see no reason why you should not get these proceedings published, especially if you do it at your own expense.

"I now declare The Dreamers adjourned *sine die!*"

"Not much !" cried the members, unanimously. "Where's your contribution ?"

"Out with it, William !" shouted Tom Snobbe. "I can tell by the set of your coat that you've got a manuscript concealed in your pocket."

"There's nothing ruins the set of a coat more quickly than a rejected manuscript in the pocket," put in Hudson Rivers. "I've been there myself — so, as Lang Tammas said, Billy, 'Pit it oot, and get it crackit.'"

"Well," Jones replied, with a pleased smile, "to tell you the truth, gentlemen, I had come prepared in case I was called upon ; but the hour is late," he added, after the manner of one who, though willing, enjoyed being persuaded. "Perhaps we had better postpone—"

"Out with it, old man. It is late, but it will be later still if you don't hurry up and begin," said Tenafly Paterson.

"Very well, then, here goes," said Jones. "Mine is a ghost-story, gentlemen, and it is called 'The Involvular Club ; or, The Return of the Screw.' It is, like the rest of the work this evening, imitative, after a fashion, but I think it will prove effective."

Mr. Jones hereupon took the manuscript from his bulging pocket and read as follows :

230

MR. JONES BEGINS

CONCLUSION

THE INVOLVULAR CLUB; OR, THE RE-
TURN OF THE SCREW

The story had taken hold upon us as we
sat round the blazing hearth of Lord Ormont's smoking-room, at Castle Aminta,
and sufficiently interfered with our comfort, as indeed from various points of
view, not to specify any one of the many,
for they were, after all, in spite of their
diversity, of equal value judged by any
standard, not even excepting the highest,
that of Vereker's disturbing narrative of
the uncanny visitor to his chambers, which
the reader may recall — indeed, must recall if he ever read it, since it was the
most remarkable ghost-story of the year
—a year in which many ghost-stories of
wonderful merit, too, were written—and
by which his reputation was made — or
rather extended, for there were a certain
few of us, including Feverel and Vanderbank and myself, who had for many years
known him as a constant—almost too constant, some of us ventured, tentatively

perhaps, but not the less convincedly, to say — producer of work of a very high order of excellence, rivalling in some of its more conspicuous elements, as well as in its minor, to lay no stress upon his subtleties, which were marked, though at times indiscreetly inevident even to the keenly analytical, hinging as these did more often than not upon abstractions born only of a circumscribed environment —circumscribed, of course, in the larger sense which means the narrowing of a circle of appreciation down to the select few constituting its essence—the productions of the greatest masters of fictional style the world has known, or is likely, in view of present tendencies towards miscalled romance, which consists solely of depicting scenes in which bloodshed and murder are rife, soon to know again—it was proper it should, in a company chosen as ours had been from among the members of The Involvular Club, with Adrian Feverel at its head, Vereker as its vice-president, and Lord Ormont, myself, and a

234

CONCLUSION

number of ladies, including Diana of the
Crossways, and little Maisie—for the child
was one of our cares, her estate was so
pitiable a one — Rhoda Fleming, Daisy
Miller, and Princess Cassimassima, one
and all, as the reader must be aware, per-
sonages—if I may thus refer to a group
of appreciation which included myself—
who knew a good thing when they saw it,
which, it may as well be confessed at
once, we rarely did in the raucous fields
of fiction outside of, though possibly at
times moderately contiguous to, our own
territory, although it should be said that
Miss Miller occasionally manifested a
lamentable lack of regard for the objects
for which The Involvular was formed, by
showing herself, in her semi - American
way, regrettably direct of speech and giv-
en over not infrequently to an unhappy
use of slang, which we all, save Maisie,
who was young, and, in spite of all she
knew, not quite so knowledgeable a young
person as some superficial observers have
chosen to believe, sincerely deprecated,
235

and on occasion when it might be done tactfully, endeavored to mitigate by a reproving glance, or by a still deeper plunge into nebulous rhetoric, as a sort of palliation to the Muse of Obscurity, which in our hearts we felt that good goddess would accept, strove to offset.

[" Excuse me," said Mr. Tom Snobbe, rising and interrupting the reader at this point, "but is that all one sentence, Mr. Jones ?"

" Yes," Jones replied. " Why not ? It's perfectly clear in its meaning. Aren't you used to long sentences on the Hudson ?" he added, sarcastically.

" No," retorted Snobbe ; " that is to say, not where I live. I believe they have 'em at Sing Sing occasionally. But they never get used to them, I'm told."

" Be quiet, Tom," said Harry Snobbe. " It's bad form to interrupt. Let Billy finish his story." Mr. Jones then resumed his manuscript.]

A perceptible shudder ran through, or rather rolled over, the group, for it was

CONCLUSION

corrugating in its quality, bringing for-
cibly to mind, quite as much for its chill,
too, as for the wrinkling suggestion of its
passage up and down our backs, turned as
some of these were towards the fire, and
others towards the steam-radiator, which
now and again clicked startlingly in the
dull red glow of the hearth light, aug-
menting the all too obvious nervousness
of the listeners, the impassive and unin-
spiring squares of iron of which certain
modern architects of a limited decorative
sense—if, indeed, they have any at all, for
the mere use of corrugated iron in the
construction of a façade would seem not
to admit of an æsthetic side to its design-
er's nature, however ornately distributed
over the surface of an exterior it may
be — have chosen to avail themselves,
prompted either by an appalling par-
simony on the part of a client, or for
reasons of haste employed for the lack
of more immediately available material, it
being an undeniable fact that in some
portions of the world stucco and terra-

cotta, now frequently used in lieu of more substantial, if not more enduring materials, are difficult of access, and the use of a speedily obtainable substitute becoming thus a requirement as inevitable as it is to be regretted, as in the case of the fruit-market at Venice, standing as it does on the bank of the Grand Canal, a pile of stark, staring, obtrusive, wrinkling zinc thrusting itself brazenly into the line of a vision attuned to the most gloriously towering palazzos, as rich in beauty as in romance, with such self-sufficiency as to bring tears to the eyes of the most stolidly unappreciative, of the most coldly unæsthetic, or, in short, as some one has chosen to say, in an essay the title of which and the name of whose author escape us at this moment, with such complacent vulgarity as to amount to nothing less than a dastardly blot upon the escutcheon of the Venetians, which all of their glorious achievements in art, in history, and in letters can never quite ineradically efface, and alongside of which the whistling steam-tugs with their belching funnels, which are by slow degrees supplanting the romantic gondolier with his picturesque costume and his tender songs of sunny climes in the cab service of the Bride of the Adriatic, seem quite excusable, or, in any event, not so unforgivable as to constitute what the Americans would call an infernal shame.

[At this point the reader was interrupted again.

"Hold on a minute, Billy—will you, please?" said Tenafly Paterson. "Let's get this story straight. As I understand the first sentence somebody told a ghost-story, didn't he?"

"Yes," replied Jones, a trifle annoyed.

"And the second sentence means that those who heard it felt creepy?"

"Precisely."

"Then why the deuce couldn't you have said, 'When So-and-So had finished, the company shuddered'?"

"Because," replied Jones, "I am reading a story which is constructed after the

manner of a certain school. I'm not reading a postal-card or a cable message."

The reader then resumed.]

Miss Miller, to relieve the strain upon
the nerves of those present, which was
becoming unbearably tense—and, in fact,
poor Maisie had burst into tears with the
sheer terror of the climax, and had been
taken off to be put to bed by Mrs. Brooken-
ham, who, in spite of many other qualities, was still a womanly woman at heart,
and not wholly deficient in those little
tendernesses, those trifling but ineffable
softnesses of nature, which are at once the
chief source of woman's strength and of
her weakness, a fact she was constantly
manifesting to us during our stay at Lord
Ormont's, and which we all remarked and
in some cases commented upon, since the
discovery had in it some of the qualities
of a revelation—began to sing one of those
extraordinary popular songs that one hears
at the music-halls in London, and in the
politer and more refined circles of American society, if indeed there may be said to

CONCLUSION

be such a thing in a land so new as to be as yet mostly veneer, with little that is solid in its social substructure, beginning as its constituent factors do at the top and working downward, rather than choosing the more natural course of beginning at the bottom and working upward, and which must materially, one may think, affect the social solidarity of the nation by retarding its growth and in otherwise interfering with its healthy, not to say normal development, and which, as the words and import of it come back to me, was known by the rather vulgar and vernacular title of "All Coons Look Alike to Me," thus indicating that the life treated of in the melody, which was not altogether unmusical, and was indeed as a matter of fact quite fetching in its quality, running in one's ears for days and nights long after its first hearing, was that of the negro, and his personal likeness to his other black brethren in the eyes even of one who was supposed to have been at one time, prior to the action of the song if not coincidently with it, the object of his affections.

[Had Jones not been wholly absorbed in the reading of this wonderful story, he might at this moment have heard a slight but unmistakable rumbling sound, and have looked up and seen much that would have interested him. But, as this kind of a story requires for its complete comprehension a complete concentration of mind, he did not hear, and so, continuing, did not see.]

Diana was the first to mitigate the silence with comment [he read] a silence whose depth had only been rendered the more depressing by Miss Miller's uncalled-for intrusion upon our mood of something that smacked of a society towards which most of us, in so far as we were able to do so, had always cultivated a strenuous aloofness, prompted not by any whelmful sense of our own perfection, latent or obvious, but rather by a realization on our part that it lacked the essentials that could make of it an interesting part of the lives

242

HE DID NOT SEE

of a group given over wholly, or at least as nearly wholly as the exiguities of existence would permit of a persistent and continuous devotion, to the contemplation of the beautiful in art, letters, or any other phase of human endeavor.

"And did his soul never thaw?" Diana asked.

"Never," replied Vanderbank, "It is frozen yet."

<hr />

Here the rumbling sound grew to such volume that, absorbed as he was in his reading, Jones could no longer fail to hear it. Lowering his manuscript, he looked sternly upon the company. The rumbling sound was a chorus, not unmusical, of snores.

The Dreamers slept.

"Well, I'll be hanged!" cried Jones, angrily, and then he walked over and looked behind the screen where the stenographer was seated. "I'll finish it if it takes all night," he muttered. "Just take this down," he added to the stenographer; but that worthy never stirred or made reply. *He too was sleeping.*

Jones muttered angrily to himself.

"Very well," he said. "I'll read it to myself, then," and he began again. For ten minutes he continued, and then on a sudden his voice faltered; his head fell forward upon his chest, his knees collapsed beneath him, and he slid inert, and snoring himself, into his chair. The MS. fluttered to the floor, and an hour later the waiters entering the room found the club unanimously engaged in dreaming once more.

The Involvular Club was too much for them, even for the author of it, but whether this was because of the lateness of the hour or because of the intricacies of the author's style I have never been able to ascertain, for Mr. Jones is very sore on the point, and therefore reticent, and as for the others, I cannot find that any of them remember enough about it to be able to speak intelligently on the subject.

THE STENOGRAPHER SLEPT

CONCLUSION

All I do know is what the landlord tells me, and that is that at 5 A.M. thirteen cabs containing thirteen sleeping souls pursued their thirteen devious ways to thirteen different houses, thus indicating that the Dreamers were ultimately adjourned, and, as they have not met since, I presume the adjournment was, as usual, *sine die.*

THE END

www.ingramcontent.com/pod-product-compliance
Lightning Source LLC
Chambersburg PA
CBHW050409260626
47156CB00003B/930